Well crafted and very scary – *T..* the

'Cool, deadpan, a rollercoaster ride to hell' – *Guardian*

'Tough, composed and about as noir as you can go. Starr is a worthy successor to Charles Willeford' – *Literary Review*

'Tough, dark, elegant, pure 90s noir' – **Edward Bunker**

'At the cutting edge of the revival of classic American noir fiction' – *Daily Telegraph*

Nothing Personal
'Original modern noir tale reminiscent of Jim Thompson or David Goodis' – *Irish Times*

'Diabolically well-plotted noir thriller... Gentle readers should take heed' – *Literary Review*

'Wholly satisfying. *Nothing Personal* is a fast, well-paced and well-plotted domestic crime thriller' – *Barcelona Review*

'The King of Noir is back. It doesn't get any darker or funnier than this... The best novel of the year' – *Bookends*

Fake ID
'Bang up-to-date, but reminiscent of David Goodis and Jim Thompson, *Fake ID* is a powerful novel of the American Dream turning into the American Nightmare that marks Starr out as a writer to follow' – *Time Out*

Also by Jason Starr

Cold Caller
Nothing Personal
Fake ID
Tough Luck
Twisted City
Lights Out
The Follower
Panic Attack
Savage Lane

Hard Feelings

JASON STARR

NO EXIT PRESS

This edition published in 2015
by No Exit Press,
an imprint of Oldcastle Books
PO Box 394, Harpenden,
Herts, AL5 1XJ, UK

noexit.co.uk
@NoExitPress

A CIP catalogue record for this book is available from the
British Library.

ISBN
978-1-84344-523-4 (print)
978-1-84344-524-1 (epub)
978-1-84344-525-8 (kindle)
978-1-84344-526-5 (pdf)

Typeset 11pt Palatino
by Avocet Typeset, Somerton, Somerset TA11 6RT
Printed in Great Britain by Clays Ltd, St Ives plc

For more information about Crime Fiction go to @CrimeTimeUK

For Ion Mills

1

Waiting to cross Fifth Avenue and Forty-eighth Street, I spotted Michael Rudnick, a guy who grew up across the street from me in Brooklyn. He was standing at the front of the crowd on the opposite corner in a black business suit and dark sunglasses, looking in my direction, but apparently not noticing me. He had changed so much since the last time I'd seen him – about twenty-two years ago, when I was twelve and he was seventeen – I guess it was incredible that I recognized him at all. He used to be overweight with horrible acne and frizzy brown hair. Now he was tall, tan, and muscular and his thick dark hair was slicked back with gel.

The DON'T WALK sign changed to WALK and the crowds from the two corners converged. When Michael and I were a few feet apart, I was still looking right at him, waiting to see if he would notice me. He was walking straight ahead, his eyes focused on something in the distance. Then, just as we were about to pass, my shoulder accidentally knocked against his and we stopped in the middle of the crowd. I saw my reflection in his sunglasses – two pale faces staring back at me. I was about to say hello when he grunted in an angry, annoyed way and continued across the street.

"Asshole," I muttered.

At the corner, I turned around to see if he was looking back, but he was gone. He must have already disappeared in the crowd heading toward the West Side.

After I said hi to Raymond, the evening doorman, I retrieved my mail – all bills – and rode the elevator to the fifth floor. When I entered my apartment, Otis started to bark.

"Shut up!" I yelled, but the hyper cocker spaniel continued to yap away, clawing against my legs.

I took Otis for his usual walk along East Sixty-Fourth Street, then I returned to the apartment, where I sat slumped on the couch in my underwear, staring at the TV, obsessing about my day at work.

This afternoon I'd had a meeting with Tom Carlson. Carlson was a CFO and decision maker for a hundred-user computer network at an insurance company in midtown. He was running an old-version Novell network and was looking to upgrade to Windows NT and purchase new PCs and servers. It was the third meeting I'd had with him and I should have left his office with nothing less than a signed contract, but when the moment came to close the sale I hesitated and the son of a bitch slipped through my fingers again. Now I would have to call him tomorrow – always a low-percentage way to close business – and try to get him to fax me a signed contract. Carlson was by far my best prospect and if he got away I had no idea what I'd do.

At around eight-thirty, I was still on the couch, ruminating in front of the TV, when Paula entered the apartment in pumps and one of her designer suits. She bent over the couch and kissed me hello, then asked how my day was. Before I could say "horrible," she said, "I have some great news – I'll tell you in a sec," and she went toward the bedroom with Otis trailing her, wagging his tail and barking.

I knew what the "great news" was. Paula's sister in San Francisco was due to give birth next week and she must have delivered early.

A few minutes later, Paula returned to the living room, wearing shorts and a long T-shirt. Like me, she had been neglecting the gym for the past few years. She used to be thin with toned muscles, but since she had stopped working out she had put on about thirty pounds. She was constantly talking about how she was fat and needed to lose weight, but I thought she looked better heavier – more feminine, anyway. Recently, she had cut her long, straight blond hair to a short bob. Whenever she asked, I told her that the cut flattered her face, making her cheekbones more prominent, but the truth was I missed her long hair.

"So," she said, "you want to hear my news?"

"Kathy had a boy."

"Guess again."

"A girl."

"She's not due for another week."

"I give up."

"Come on, Rich, this is important."

I shut off the TV with the remote.

"I got a promotion," she said, smiling.

"Really?"

"Isn't it unbelievable? I thought for sure Brian would get it – I mean the way Brian and Chris are so buddy-buddy. But Chris called me into his office this afternoon and gave me the great news – you're looking at the new VP of equity research."

"Wow," I said, trying to sound enthusiastic.

"I can't tell you what a relief this is," Paula said. "For the past few weeks, my job's been so crazy – I mean working on three reports at once and then having this promotion hanging over me. I just wanted it to be resolved one way or another, but to have it turn out this way is just incredible. You know this means I'll get a salary increase, too."

"Great."

"My base'll be seventy a year now."

Ten more than my base, I thought.

"That really is terrific news," I said.

"I think it'll really take some pressure off us now. Maybe we could put a little away in savings, pay off the credit cards…"

"We'll have to go out this weekend and celebrate."

"You want to go out to dinner right now? Come on,

I'll change into some clothes – I could be ready in ten minutes."

"I really don't feel like it tonight."

"Come on, when was the last time we went out to dinner? Let's go to that new Vietnamese place on Third. It's beautiful out. We could sit at a table outside, order a bottle of wine –"

"I said I'm not in the mood."

I was looking away but I could sense Paula staring at me. Finally, she said, "What's wrong?"

"Nothing."

"You don't seem very happy to see me tonight."

"I'm just tired."

"You don't seem very happy about my promotion, either."

"*What?*" I said, as if that were totally ridiculous. "What are you talking about? I'm thrilled you were promoted, but I don't feel like going out to dinner. Is there something wrong with that?"

I turned on the TV again and started flipping stations. Paula sat next to me on the couch, Indian-style, staring blankly at the screen. I could tell she was still angry at me, but I didn't feel like fighting anymore.

Finally, I said, "So how is Kathy, anyway?"

"We have to talk, Richard."

"Not now."

"You've been acting strange lately – the past few weeks anyway. You've been very distant, keeping everything to yourself. I think it's starting to affect the marriage."

I hated when Paula referred to us as "the marriage," and how she was always trying to analyze me. She had been seeing a shrink once a week for the past five years and she was always telling me that I wasn't expressing myself or that I was being "passive-aggressive" or "projecting" or "displacing my emotions" or whatever psychobabble she could come up with.

"I'm really not in the mood for this right now," I said on my way into the kitchen.

Following me she said, "See? This is exactly what I'm talking about."

I took a menu for Chinese food out from one of the counter drawers. Last year we'd had the kitchen redone – installing the snack bar, putting down new tiles, refacing the cabinets. Home improvements and Paula's work wardrobe were the major reasons we had over twenty thousand dollars in credit-card debt.

"You can't just walk away," Paula said. "When something's bothering you, you have to talk about it."

"How about shrimp with lobster sauce?"

"You're upset I got promoted," she said. "It threatens your male ego – makes the hunter feel like he's not providing."

"Stop trying to analyze me, all right?" I said. "I'm ordering. You want something or not?"

"Why don't you just admit that you resent my promotion?"

"I'm getting you moo shu chicken."

I ordered the food in the living room. Paula entered and stood facing me with her hands on her hips.

"Admit it," she said.

"Admit what?"

"That you want me to make less money than you."

"That's ridiculous," I said. "The more money you make the better. Make two hundred a year, make three hundred! The way things are going for me, we may need all the money we can get."

Otis started barking again. I yelled "Shut up!" then I sat down on the couch. Paula sat next to me, waited a few seconds, then said, "How did your big sales meeting go today?"

"How the hell do you think it went?"

She rested her hand on my lap.

"I'm sorry," she said. "Maybe you should think about quitting."

"What the hell are you talking about?" I was uncomfortable with her hand on me so I stood up. "You think I can just go in there tomorrow and quit? That'll look great on my résumé – seven months at the job without making a sale. That'll sound really great when I start interviewing."

"It's not your fault –"

"Then whose fault is it?"

"There're lots of explanations you can give," Paula said. "The company was restructuring, you had personal differences with your supervisors..."

"They can smell that bullshit a mile away."

"But you don't have to put all this pressure on yourself," Paula said, "that's only going to make things worse. Now that I've gotten my raise –"

"So you're getting, what, another fifteen K a year? After taxes, what's that, eight or nine grand? Whoop-de-fucking-doo. Have you seen our credit-card bills lately? Face it, we're living paycheck to fucking paycheck. What happens the next time we want to renovate? Or what about moving out of the city someday? Maybe you'd like to just sell this place, take the hundred-grand loss."

"Oh, stop with this bullshit," Paula said, standing up. "Just because you had a bad day doesn't mean you have to take it out on me. I got some great news today and you obviously don't give a shit."

Paula marched into the bedroom and slammed the door. Otis was barking again. I threw a couch cushion – it hit Otis's ass and ricocheted onto the floor. He barked once, defiantly, then scurried meekly into the kitchen.

I sat on the couch with my head in my hands until the Chinese food arrived. Then I knocked on the bedroom door and apologized for losing my temper. About a minute later, Paula joined me at the dining room table.

We ate, barely talking. She left over most of her dish and announced she had a headache.

"Maybe there's MSG in the food," I said. "I forgot to order it without."

"No, it's just my usual migraine. I have to go lie down."

Paula went back to the bedroom. I cleaned up from dinner then I took Otis for his walk, down the block and back. When I returned to the apartment Paula was asleep in bed.

"Sorry about before," I whispered, leaning over her.

"It's okay," she said, half-asleep.

"Feeling better?"

"Little bit," she said.

"I'm really sorry. I shouldn't've taken my work out on you. I'm very happy you got your promotion. I really think it's great news and I want to take you out tomorrow night to celebrate."

"Okay," she said.

"How's around seven?"

"That's fine."

"Goodnight, honey." I kissed her lips.

"Goodnight," she mumbled, turning onto her side.

After I washed up I got into bed next to Paula and read a few chapters of *How to Be a Bulldog*, the latest book on sales strategy that I'd placed on my night table. Suddenly exhausted, I rested the book on my chest and closed my eyes. I remembered passing Michael Rudnick on Fifth Avenue earlier, then I saw myself as a ten- or eleven-year-old in front of my old house on Stratford Road in Brooklyn. I was alone, bouncing a basketball on the sidewalk, when a teenaged Michael Rudnick appeared. He was overweight, with his usual faceful of acne. He had very thick eyebrows that grew together above his nose and some older kids on the block had nicknamed him "The Caterpillar." Michael asked me if I wanted to play Ping-Pong with him in his basement. He was one of the "big kids" on my block, in high school, and whenever he invited me to play Ping-Pong it made me feel special. "Sure," I said excitedly. "Let's go!" Michael's parents weren't home, and his house was dark and empty. We went down to the cold, musty basement and I watched as Michael adjusted the net on the Ping-Pong table. Then he explained the rules of the game – if I won I'd get five dollars, if he won he'd get to give me a wedgie. I didn't really understand the trade-off, but I went along with it anyway. Of course, the odds were stacked in his favor because he was a much better Ping-Pong player than I was. He was destroying me – winning almost every point. He needed one point to win and when my shot missed the end of the table he put down his paddle and yelled, "You're gonna feel it!" Laughing hysterically, thinking it was part of the "game," I ran away until he caught me from behind and immediately reached around my waist and started yanking up the elastic band of my underwear. The wedgie was painful, but I was still laughing. I didn't like what he was doing to me, but I was afraid if I complained he'd stop inviting me to his basement to play Ping-Pong. He was much taller and stronger than me, and he was pulling so hard he was lifting me off the ground. "Stop, stop!" I yelled, but still laughing, still thinking we were playing a game. Then he moved me toward the sofa. I was still squirming, trying to get away, my face pressed against the sticky black vinyl. I didn't know why he was doing this – why he thought it was so much fun. I was facedown on the couch and he was on top of me, grunting and sweating.

I opened my eyes suddenly, my pulse throbbing as if I had just run a full sprint. Paula was fast asleep next to me, snoring softly. I got out of bed. Otis tried to follow me, but I closed the bedroom door ahead of him and went into the kitchen.

Standing in front of the open refrigerator, I gulped down

orange juice straight from the container. I needed fresh air.
I went through the living room, out to the terrace.

It was a warm, muggy night and there wasn't much air
to breathe. As I leaned against the railing, looking down at
the busy Third Avenue traffic, I heard Michael Rudnick's
high-pitched voice shouting, "You're gonna feel it! You're
gonna feel it!" as clearly as if he were on the terrace next to
me. I could still feel the weight of his body on top of mine,
feeling trapped and claustrophobic underneath him, and
I remembered the nauseating smell of – probably his
father's – cheap cologne.

I went back into the apartment and locked the terrace
door. In the bathroom, I splashed my face with cold water.
I remembered reading an article in the *Times* about how
some people blocked out traumatic memories from their
childhoods and then suddenly remembered them years
later. But it was hard to believe that something like this
might have happened to me.

When I lay down in bed, Paula stirred.

"Where were you?"

"The terrace."

"Why?"

"To get some fresh air."

"You okay, sweetie?"

"Yeah."

"Sure?"

"Positive."

"Sorry about before."

"Me, too."

But, the truth was, I'd forgotten what we had been
fighting about.

2

Paula slid open the shower door. I hadn't heard her come into the bathroom and the noise jarred me from my thoughts.

"I'm leaving for work," she said.

"Wait."

I rinsed the soap off my face then kissed her. I knew I had acted like a jerk last night and I wanted to make up for it.

"Remember," I said, "I want to take you out to dinner tonight to celebrate your promotion."

"Okay," she said. "That sounds like fun."

"How about I make a reservation for seven?"

"Better make it seven-thirty. I'll call if I'm going to be late."

She said goodbye again, then I slid the shower door closed. Usually, Paula left for work around seven, but it was only about six-twenty now. I figured she was getting an early start to make a good impression.

Paula had worked very hard to get ahead – going to school at night for three years to finish her MBA, then kissing ass and working long hours to climb the corporate ladder. I knew how much the promotion to VP meant to Paula and tonight I was planning to give her the celebration she deserved.

I left the apartment at about seven-fifteen. I usually walked to work along the same route – down Third Avenue to Forty-eighth Street, then across town to Sixth Avenue. Once in a while – usually during bad weather or on cold winter days – I took cabs, but I never took public transportation.

After using my swipe card to unlock the front door, I entered my office at a little before eight o'clock. I picked

18

up my interoffice cellphone at the desk, then went down the long corridor, by the secretaries' cubicles, to my office in the sales department.

At my old job at Network Strategies, where my title had been merely salesman, I'd had a big corner office with a spectacular view of the East River. Now, as a senior salesman at Midtown Consulting, I was crammed into a narrow, stuffy office with a single window facing the back of a building. I missed the prestige of a corner office. When you have one of the biggest, most luxurious offices at a company, you get special treatment. In the hallways or at the water cooler, people smile at you and ask you how your weekend was or whether you've seen any good movies lately. Or they might offer to help you at the copy machine, or ask you if they can pick up anything when they're on their way to the deli. But now people barely paid attention to me. Sometimes when I was walking in the hallway I would smile at someone and they would look back at me with a blank face, as if I were invisible.

Lately, I'd been regretting the decision I'd made seven months ago to leave my old job. When the offer came from the headhunter I had been at Network Strategies for nearly six years and I'd had no intention of quitting. Then I was offered this incredible package at Midtown, with a sixty-a-year base salary and better benefits. Usually, I hung up on headhunters, but that day I listened.

At the time, there was no way of knowing that coming to Midtown Consulting would probably be the worst decision of my career.

I followed my typical morning routine – turning on my PC, checking my email and voicemail – then I went to the coffee machine to get a cup of black coffee with three sugars. Back at my desk, I logged on to a Lotus Notes scheduling program. I had no out-of-office appointments today, but there were a number of important callbacks I needed to make this morning, including to Tom Carlson, the CFO I had met with yesterday afternoon.

I dialed Carlson's number, expecting to reach his secretary, but on the second ring he answered.

"Good morning, Tom," I said, trying to sound as upbeat as possible.

"Who's this?"

"Richard Segal – Midtown Consulting. How are you today?"

After a long pause he said, "Ah ha."

"Great, thanks for asking," I said. "The reason I'm calling, Tom, is yesterday I didn't get a chance to tell you – we can knock an additional two percent off that quote, which should save your company an additional twenty or thirty thousand dollars over the course of the contract and –"

"Yeah, I didn't really get a chance to look that over yet," he interrupted. "I'll call you when I'm ready, okay?"

"If there's anything you don't understand, Tom, or need clarification on I'd be delighted –"

"Didn't I tell you yesterday that I'd call you when I was ready to make a decision?"

"Yes, but I thought you'd want to know –"

"You know, I feel like you're trying to talk me into doing something I don't want to do," he said, "and I don't like having that feeling."

"I'm sorry if I gave you that impression, Tom," I said. "But the real reason –"

"Look, why don't we just forget the whole thing?"

"I... Excuse me?"

"I've decided I want to take my business elsewhere."

"I don't understand," I said, unable to hide my frustration anymore. "I mean yesterday... at the meeting –"

"We're going to accept an offer from another firm, all right?"

"But did you have a chance to look over our quote yet?"

"I'm not interested in your quote."

Now I couldn't control myself.

"Then why the hell did you agree to meet with me yesterday?"

"The truth? I forgot about the damn meeting until you showed up. Look, the answer is no, thank you very much. Goodbye."

Carlson hung up. Stunned, I held the receiver against my ear until the line started beeping, then I replaced it. I was still in shock. I couldn't believe that all the months I'd spent working on the Carlson account had come to absolutely nothing.

I closed my eyes and let out a long, deep breath. Then I took a swig of coffee and kept going.

I reached several voicemails then, finally, I got a hold of Rajid Hamir, an MIS manager at Prudential I had been trying to reach for the past few weeks.

"Hello, Rajid, this is Richard Segal at Midtown Consulting."

"Who?"

"Richard Segal," I said slowly. "Remember – we met last month and I gave you a quote a few weeks ago for those two NT consultants you were looking for?"

"Sorry, we have no budget for that now," he said. "Try again next quarter."

When I tried to schedule an advance appointment for next quarter, Rajid hung up on me.

I made about a dozen more calls, finally reaching another prospect. But the guy said he was using another consulting firm right now, to call back next year. I dialed number after number with no success.

Staring at the computer screen, I was suddenly exhausted and I was starting to get a headache. I went down the hallway into the kitchen area and poured myself another cup of coffee. A voice behind me said, "Hey, Richie, how's it goin'?"

I looked over my shoulder and saw the smiling face

of Steve Ferguson. Steve was also a senior salesman at Midtown, but I'd always thought he belonged selling shoes instead of computer networks. Last month, for the second month in a row, he was Midtown's salesman of the month, closing nearly half a million dollars of new business.

"I'm all right," I said, adding a third sugar to my coffee. "How about you?"

"Got laid last night so I can't complain," Steve said, smiling out of the corner of his mouth. Then he slapped me on the back and said, "So how're the sales coming along?"

"All right," I said, hating his guts.

"Yeah? Did you close that MHI account yet?"

"No, not yet," I said, putting a lid over the coffee.

"You've been working on that one for a while, haven't you? What's holding it up?"

"Just waiting for the signed contract."

I stepped around him, trying to end the conversation, but he walked next to me, following me out of the kitchen.

"So I closed that Chase deal I was working on," he said as if I'd asked him how his sales were coming.

"That's great," I said.

"Yeah, four consultants, nine-month project – you know, a tiny one. Should get me some nice commish, though. There's also some other projects in the works – hopefully it'll lead to something ongoing. Did you hear about the Everson deal?"

"No," I said.

"Yeah, it's this new-media ad agency on Forty-second. Got the signed contract in the mail yesterday – three-fifty K. Hey, if you need any help closing that MHI account, I'm here to help you, man. Seriously, if you want me to throw a call for you, come to a meeting – anything I can do. I know how important it is to get that first sale under your belt."

"Thanks, I'll think about it," I said, fake smiling.

In front of his office – a corner office – Steve stopped

walking and said, "So I guess I'll see you at the ten o'clock."

I stopped.

"What ten o'clock?"

"Didn't you get the memo from Bob about the sales meeting today?"

"No."

"Oh. Well, guess I'll catch you later."

When I got back to my office I checked my email log, but there was no message from Bob about any ten o'clock meeting. I called one of the guys at the help desk, figuring there must be a problem with my email, but they said the system was fine.

I went down the hallway to the cubicles where Midtown's three junior salesmen worked. Peter Rabinowitz and Rob Cohen were busy on the phone, but John Hennessy was working at his PC. John was clean cut, in his mid-twenties, working at his first or second job out of college.

"Hi, John," I said.

"Richard," he said, "how's it going?"

"Not bad, not bad," I said. "Did you get a memo about a ten o'clock sales meeting?"

"Yes, sir," he said, "Will I see you there?"

"Maybe," I said. "I might be busy with a client."

As a final possibility, I wondered if Heidi, Bob's secretary, had forgotten to send me the memo. I called her and asked her to hold my calls for the next couple of hours because I was going to be working in my office, figuring if I was supposed to attend a meeting she would tell me. But she agreed to take my calls without another word.

I had seen this happen before at previous jobs and I knew exactly what it meant. When an employee, especially a senior employee, was suddenly shut out of meetings he'd better get his résumé ready because he was as good as gone.

I called more leads from my database, determined to make *something* happen. But after two hours of nearly nonstop dialing I had zero success. I was starting to feel dizzy and light-headed when I saw myself in Michael Rudnick's basement and heard his teenaged voice shouting, "You're gonna feel it! You're gonna feel it!" Like last night, my heart was racing. Fuck, this was all I needed in my life right now.

I tried to get back to work, but I couldn't get Michael Rudnick out of my head. I wondered if it was really him I had passed on the street yesterday. The guy I'd seen seemed too thin and fit to be Rudnick, and his skin looked too perfect. His "caterpillar" eyebrow would have been a dead giveaway, but yesterday his eyebrows had been hidden by dark sunglasses.

I logged on to the internet and did a "people search" for "Michael Rudnick" in Manhattan. The search returned two hits, a "Michael L. Rudnick" with an address on Washington Street and a "Michael J. Rudnick, Esquire" with an address on Madison Avenue. Michael J. Rudnick, the lawyer, seemed like the best possibility because the address – probably of an office – was around where I had seen him waiting to cross the street yesterday evening. Besides, the idea of Michael Rudnick as a lawyer made a lot of sense. As a teenager, he was controlling, arrogant, self-centered – all prerequisites for a career in law. "Lawyer" also fit the impression I had gotten of him on the street corner – wealthy, successful, very self-confident about his appearance and his status. I also remembered the way he had grunted at me after we knocked shoulders, as if I were beneath him and inconsequential. But I definitely couldn't see him as a trial lawyer. No, a guy like him would do something more impersonal. He was probably a tax attorney.

It was nearing noon and no one had come to my office to tell me that I was missing a sales meeting. Realizing that I hadn't eaten anything all day, I decided to grab a bite then come back to the office and hit the phones again.

I went to the pizza place I sometimes went to for lunch on Seventh Avenue. It wasn't particularly good pizza, but what did I care? Usually, I wolfed down my lunches so fast that I could be eating cardboard with tomato sauce and rubber cheese and I wouldn't know the difference.

I sat with my two slices at a table in the back, swallowing my bites half-chewed, obsessing about my shitty morning and my even shittier life. I'd always thought that, by the time I was in my mid-thirties, I'd be happily married, living in a big house in the suburbs, with two kids and plenty of money in the bank. Maybe Paula and I had spent too much in our twenties, taking those extravagant vacations to the Bahamas and Hawaii. Unlike everyone else in the world who seemed to be striking it rich in the stock market, we were broke. Our apartment was worth half of what we'd paid for it, thanks to a major building assessment, and except for our retirement funds we had almost no money saved, which was ridiculous for a couple our age. And then there were the credit-card bills and the utility bills and the new expenses that always seemed to be popping up. Of course, we could sell the apartment for a loss now, maybe rent a smaller place for a few years until our bills were paid. But we needed the tax break that we got from ownership and the rental would probably wind up costing the same as or more than we were paying now.

I couldn't finish my second slice. I left the pizza place and reemerged on Seventh Avenue. The air was thick and smoggy. It had been drizzling earlier – now the sky was clearing. I walked mindlessly for a while, then I stopped, realizing that I was on the corner of Fifth Avenue and Forty-eighth Street, the same corner where I had seen Michael Rudnick yesterday. The corner was several blocks from the pizza place and I had no idea why I had walked there.

From my office, I called Maison, a French restaurant on Second Avenue, and made a dinner reservation for seven-thirty. I had never eaten there before, but Paula loved French food and I wanted to take her someplace special to celebrate her promotion.

I started making sales calls again, still getting nowhere. At around two-thirty, I got a call from Heidi, saying that Bob wanted to see me right away. I asked her what it was about and she said she had no idea.

When I entered Bob's office and saw him, sitting at his desk, staring at his computer monitor with a very serious expression, I figured he must have made the decision to fire me. I envisioned breaking the news to Paula tonight, then having to check the help wanteds on Sunday.

"Take a seat," Bob said without looking at me.

Naturally, as president of the company, Bob had a huge corner office. I could see a sliver of Central Park through the north-facing window behind his desk, and the towering GE Building at Rockefeller Center to the east.

Bob was short – about five-six – and he covered the large bald spot on the center of his head with a black yarmulke. He always wore what looked like the same white button-down shirt tucked into black slacks. He was in his late thirties or early forties. Sometimes when he saw me in the hallway he stopped to tell me some new joke he'd heard. I always knew that the main reason he seemed to like me, and why he had probably been reluctant to fire me, was because my last name was Segal. At my job interview, I could tell Bob had assumed that I was Jewish and I hadn't corrected him.

I sat in the cushioned seat across from his desk. For a while, he continued to stare at the computer monitor and I thought he might have forgotten I was in the room. Finally, he swiveled back toward the desk and said, "Sorry to keep you waiting. How are you?"

"Pretty good," I said.

"Getting warmer out there," he said.

"Warmer?" I said.

"The weather," he said.

"Oh, right," I said. "Yeah, it has been nice lately."

"My wife and I are opening our country house in Tuxedo soon," Bob said.

"Great," I said.

We stared at each other.

"Anyway," he said, "I just called you in here to get the status on some of your accounts – see where you are and where you're going."

"Okay," I said, relieved to hear that I wasn't going to be canned. Not yet, anyway.

"First of all, Steve told me you're pretty close to closing the Media Horizons account?"

"*Steve* said that?"

"So you're not close?"

"They're just waiting for the budget to come through," I said, giving the most obvious excuse for a delay.

"Did they give you a timetable when you can expect to hear about it?"

"A few days – maybe a week or two."

"Well, hopefully that one will come through. Are you working on anything else hot?"

"A few things," I lied.

"Good. Which ones?"

"I have a bid out for a couple of consultants, another for an outsourcing project."

My answers were smooth and confident and I knew he couldn't tell I was full of shit.

"Good – I'm glad to see you have a few irons in the fire. Hopefully, you'll close all three sales and you'll be off and running."

"That's what I'm hoping for," I said.

"But, I have to be honest with you, Richard – I don't like to hit my employees with any surprises. When I hired you to come work for me, you led me to believe you would bring some business with you. You remember that, right? And I'm sure you're aware you've been working here seven months now and you haven't made a single sale for us yet. Now, I know a lot of that is out of your control and I'm not blaming you for anything. But, at the same time, if your production doesn't increase I'm going to have to reevaluate your position here at Midtown. I know you were a big producer at your old job and I know you can do it again. I also think you're a nice guy and I hope, from the bottom of my heart, that you stay with our company for many years. But I'm also running a business here and I can't keep a salesman on, on any level, just because he's a mensch. You understand that, don't you?"

"Yes," I said.

"But don't worry, I'm sure it won't get to that point. I'm sure you'll close the three sales you just mentioned and, before you know it, I'll be giving you the award for salesman of the month. If there's anything I can do to help you succeed at this company, please tell me what it is, and I'd be delighted to do it."

"I appreciate that, but there's nothing you can do," I said. "I just need to get some signed contracts, that's all."

"Maybe you should let Steve Ferguson come with you to your next sales meeting, or go with him to one of his. I know you probably have your own techniques, but sometimes watching someone who's been successful can be very helpful."

"I don't think that'll help me," I said.

"Maybe you should try it anyway," Bob said. "You never know what might rub off on you. Hey, did you hear about the Polack who locked his keys in his car? He needed a hanger to get his family out."

I laughed politely at the dumb joke.

"By the way," Bob said as I stood up, "I don't know if

you heard, but we're going to be doing a little remodeling in the office next week."

"No, I didn't hear about that," I said.

"We need to expand our recruiting and marketing departments because a few new people are starting. The bottom line is that someone is going to lose his or her office. We haven't made a decision about who that person will be yet, but I just wanted you to be prepared. Like I said – no surprises."

I went back to my office calmly and then I slammed the door behind me, rattling the flimsy wall.

I considered calling my old boss at Network Strategies and begging for my old job back, but I knew this would be a waste of time. I hadn't left on the best of terms to begin with, and I'd really soured things by trying – unsuccessfully – to take some of my old clients with me to Midtown.

I would work on my résumé over the weekend, get back in touch with some headhunters. I didn't care if I had to take a pay cut, there was no way in hell I was moving to a cubicle.

3

At seven-fifteen Paula wasn't home from work yet. I called her office and there was no answer. She usually took cabs to and from work, so I assumed she was caught in rush-hour traffic on the FDR Drive or near the Fifty-ninth Street Bridge.

I had picked up a bouquet of long-stemmed pink roses and a card, congratulating her on her promotion. I was still in a bad mood about work, but I was determined not to take it out on Paula.

To help relax, I went to the liquor cabinet and poured myself half a glass of Scotch, and then I filled the rest of the glass with seltzer. I hadn't had a drink in a long time – maybe six months – and the first few sips gave me a nice buzz.

I had started drinking in high school. In college, at SUNY Buffalo, I drank more often and then, when I moved back to the city after graduation, I went out to bars with friends at least a few times a week. After a few embarrassing episodes when I blacked out and made a fool of myself at parties, I decided to go cold turkey.

At seven-twenty, there was still no sign of Paula. I had already called her on her cellphone, but it wasn't turned on. I tried again and it still wasn't on. I called her office and got her tape, and then I called my answering machine at work but there were no messages. I checked my watch again. It was after seven-thirty, so we were officially late for our dinner reservation.

I finished my drink and poured another.

For a while, it seemed like our marital problems were behind us, but now I wondered if I'd just been naive. Maybe I didn't want to believe it all this time, so I had blocked out the obvious signs – Paula's working late, how she was often "too tired" to make love, and how we hardly spent any time together anymore.

Five years ago, a few months after our wedding, Paula confessed she'd had an affair with Andy Connelly, an ex-boyfriend from high school. She said she was "confused" and called it "a meaningless fling." It took me a long time to forgive her, but I finally did, and for years neither of us even mentioned Andy's name. Then, a few months ago, Paula and I were leaving a restaurant on Columbus Avenue when we saw him. He was alone and he and Paula smiled at each other when they passed, but they didn't say anything. Later, in the cab home, I asked Paula why she had smiled and she said she didn't realize she had. Trying to put me at ease, she commented about how much weight Andy had gained and how he seemed to have aged twenty years.

At eight-fifteen, I was sitting at the snack bar in the kitchen, working on a third Scotch, when I heard a key turning in the lock. Otis started barking and then Paula entered the apartment.

"Hello," she said.

I didn't answer. She came into the kitchen and saw me.

"Hi," she said.

I noticed that her hair looked messy and her work suit was wrinkled. I imagined that she had been in a hotel room with Andy and had to get dressed in a hurry.

"You're late," I said.

"Late?" she said. "Late for what?"

"We had a dinner reservation."

"Oh my God, I totally forgot." She looked genuinely surprised, but she could have been faking it. "I had to meet with Chris about my new position and then I had this other meeting that ran late. But I'm sorry. Let's go right now."

"What was your meeting about?"

"I told you – my new position."

"Not that meeting. The *other* meeting. The one that ran late."

"It was a staff meeting."

"A staff meeting, huh?"

"That's right. What's this all about, anyway?"

"Nothing," I said. "I guess I'm just a little surprised you forgot about dinner, that's all."

"I said I'm sorry. What else do you want me to say?"

Paula looked at me closely, then she glanced at the rinsed-out glass on the counter, and then she examined me again.

"Have you been drinking?" she asked.

"No," I said.

"Then what's that glass doing on the counter?"

"Why was your cellphone off?"

"Excuse me?"

"Your cellphone was off. You never have it off."

"I don't know, I must've forgotten to turn it on when I left my office. I can't believe you're acting this way."

Paula started to leave the kitchen, but I stood in front of her, blocking her.

"Why is your suit wrinkled?" I asked.

"Will you get out of my way, please?"

"Were you with Andy Connelly?"

"What? Are you out of your mind?"

Paula pushed past me and left the kitchen. I stood there, suddenly feeling like an idiot. I knew Paula hadn't been with Andy Connelly. It was just the alcohol, making me paranoid. Paula had been in a late meeting and had forgotten to turn on her cellphone. These were both reasonable explanations.

I went into the dining room to get the bouquet of roses and the card, and then I opened the bedroom door and poked my head inside. Paula was sitting on the foot of the bed, taking off her shoes.

"I'm sorry," I said.

She didn't answer.

"I've been under a lot of pressure lately," I went on,

"with work and everything. I shouldn't've taken it out on you. I bought you a present."

Paula looked over and I came into the room, holding the flowers in front of me. Her face brightened momentarily. She took the flowers, resting them on the bed beside her, and said, "Thank you." Then she glanced at the card, where I had written, *Congratulations on your promotion to Vice President, to a wonderful woman and to my best friend, love always, Richard,* and said, "That's sweet." She stood up and kissed me quickly, then sat back down and started taking off her other shoe.

"Don't get undressed," I said. "I still want to take you out to dinner."

"You just accused me of having an affair."

"I said I was sorry. I was just – I'm really sorry."

"You were just what?"

"Nothing."

"You were going to say drunk, weren't you?"

"No."

"*Please.* Do you really think I'm *that* stupid? I can smell the alcohol on your breath from across the room. Why are you doing this? Am I going to have to start drawing lines on the liquor bottles like I –"

"I only had one – I swear to God."

"You said you were going to stop. You *promised.*"

"I *did* stop. I was just upset, that's all. So I had a drink – one drink. It wasn't a big deal."

"Do you still think I'm cheating on you?"

"Will you stop with that already?"

"I thought that was all over with, but if you're still –"

"I'm telling you, it's work and that's it. Come on, let's just go to dinner."

I leaned down and kissed her gently on the lips.

"All right," she said. "Just give me a few minutes to get ready."

On the way out of the building, I could tell Paula was

still upset, but when we were walking uptown to the restaurant I put my arm around her and she didn't pull away, so I knew she had forgiven me.

Even though we were late for our reservation at Maison, we were able to get a table on the sidewalk. Paula had the fluke and I had the monkfish.

In the middle of the meal I held Paula's hand and said, "I have an idea – let's go away this weekend."

"You mean tomorrow?"

"Why not? Let's go someplace quiet – not the Hamptons with that whole scene there. How about the Berkshires?"

"You serious?"

"Why not? We'll just rent a car and drive up. I don't know about you, but I really need to get the hell out of the city for a couple of days – clear my head. And it'll be nice to spend some time alone with no distractions. When was the last time we did that?"

"I guess we've both had difficult weeks," Paula said.

We had dessert – splitting a piece of chocolate soufflé cake – then we walked back to our apartment with our arms around each other.

I took Otis out for a walk while Paula got ready for bed. I came back to the apartment and went into the bedroom, where the lights were out.

"I'm waiting for you," Paula said seductively.

We hadn't made love in over a week and it was good to get back in the saddle again. Paula was more energetic than usual, digging her fingernails into my back and spending a long time on top. It was nice, I guess, but I couldn't help wondering if she was thinking about someone else.

4

The next morning, I was in my office by eight-fifteen to prepare for a ten o'clock sales meeting with Joe Fertinelli at Hutchinson Securities. At nine-fifteen, I took a cab across town and arrived at the Hutchinson building on Lexington and Thirty-fifth at around nine-thirty. I didn't want to show up at the meeting too early, so I bought a cup of coffee from a cart on the street. Caffeine was good before a sales meeting, to build up energy, but I didn't want to be overanxious, so I took a few sips then threw the rest away. At a quarter to ten, I took an elevator up to the Hutchinson office, chewing on an Altoid to get rid of my coffee breath.

As I waited in the lobby, I rehearsed to myself exactly what I wanted to say. I imagined sitting down across from Fertinelli in his office and asking him about his golf game. The last time we'd met he'd made a couple of references to golf and it was always good to give a client the impression that you considered him an *individual*, rather than just a faceless prospect you couldn't care less about. Gradually, I would segue into asking him if he had any questions about the proposal and then, very confidently and aggressively, I'd work toward the close. Maybe I'd look him in the eye and say casually, "So how about we get the ball rolling and sign?"

At ten-thirty, Fertinelli came into the lobby. He was short and thin with dark hair and a large ethnic nose. He was probably about forty or forty-five. We shook hands and I knew I was in trouble. His handshake was weak and he pulled away first, avoiding eye contact. I tried to stay positive. Sitting across from him in his office, I asked him about his golf game – which I could tell he appreciated – and then I went over the proposal with him. He told me that his boss wanted to compare my proposal to proposals from other companies before he made a decision, but I continued to pressure him politely, remembering how I'd promised myself that I'd be a bulldog closer from now on. I said, "Why don't we just get the ball rolling?" and he said, "I told you – my boss wants to see other proposals." Every salesman knows that the key to making a client say yes is to make him say no five times. So I continued to press, saying, "There's no sense waiting – why not just give me your John Hancock and we'll start work this afternoon, okey dokey?"

Finally, Fertinelli said, "Look, I really wish you'd stop pressuring me, all right? I don't like to be pressured."

On the way back to reception, he promised that he'd call me next week, but I knew he was full of shit. He wouldn't call, and when I tried to call him, he would be "in a meeting" or "away from his desk."

Walking mindlessly across town through the crowded midtown streets, I was ready to quit my job, quit my career. I was even ready to go see a shrink.

Back at my office, I passed Bob Goldstein, the last person I wanted to see, in the hallway.

"How'd the meeting go?" he asked.

"Great," I said, hoping my smile didn't look too phony. "I think I'm gonna close him Monday morning."

"Let's hope so," Bob said.

As I booted up my computer and accessed my database of leads, I decided to change my whole attitude. Struggling to make sales obviously wasn't working, so I might as well just give up, resign myself to the fact that I was a loser and a failure, and see what happened.

I spent the rest of the morning calmly calling prospects, without any expectations, and the strategy worked. I set up two appointments for next week with MIS managers I had been trying to meet with for weeks.

Sometimes it amazed me how the future could seem so hopeless at one moment and so bright at the next.

Suddenly, I was confident that everything would work out for me after all.

I left the office early, at about three-thirty, and arrived at my apartment at a little after four. Paula came home at around five. She had arranged to have a neighbor in the building take care of Otis for the weekend.

I carried the luggage down to the lobby – two small suitcases and our tennis rackets – and then I went to pick up the car that I had reserved last night. When I pulled up to the building, Paula was waiting out front. She looked especially attractive today in khaki shorts, a black T-shirt, and sunglasses on her head, pushing back her blond hair.

Driving through Westchester along the Taconic State Parkway, I opened the windows slightly, letting in a rush of cool, refreshing country air.

"By the way, you were really great last night," Paula said.

She put her hand on my thigh, kneading my leg with her fingers. I looked over and saw her giving me a sexy smile.

"So were you," I said, looking back toward the road.

I lowered the visor to shield my eyes from the setting sun.

We arrived in Stockbridge at around nine o'clock. The temperature was probably in the fifties, at least ten degrees cooler than in the city. Paula said she was cold and she walked ahead of me while I took our luggage out of the trunk.

Our reservation was at the Red Lion Inn, a quaint, eighteenth-century resort famous for its wide front porch with big white chairs facing the town's Main Street. We had stayed there once before, in the height of the summer tourist season, and had a great time. Tonight, the porch was empty and there were only a few people in the lobby, but I figured this was to be expected given the chilly weather and that it was the off-season.

Our room was so cold we had to call down for a space heater. After we unpacked, I suggested that we go downstairs for tea or coffee, but Paula said she'd rather go to bed early. I went to the bathroom and took a quick shower. When I came out, the lights were dim and Paula was lying in bed, wearing a black see-through negligee. Besides the natural surprise, seeing her in a sexy outfit was jarring. Before we were married, when we first moved in together in Manhattan, she used to dress up for me all the time, and we occasionally rented porno movies and experimented with sex toys. But lately, if we did it with the lights on it was a big deal.

"Where did you get that?" I asked.

"What do you mean?" she said. "You bought it for me."

I remembered. It was the Victoria's Secret nightie I'd bought for her to wear on our honeymoon in Jamaica.

"I didn't know you still had it."

"I would never throw it away, even though it is a little small on me now."

"Are you kidding?" I said. "It fits you perfectly. But what made you bring it up here?"

"I don't know. I found it in the drawer the other day and I thought it would be fun to wear again. But if you want me to take it off –"

"No, I think I can manage that part myself."

I took off my T-shirt and my boxers and climbed into bed. I started kissing her, my hands sliding over her breasts and hips, down her waist.

"You want a back massage?" she asked.

"Sure," I said.

I lay on my stomach and Paula sat on my lower back. It felt good at first as she gently worked out the knots in my shoulders and neck, but then she started to work my shoulders harder and suddenly I was in Michael

Rudnick's basement and I could smell the odor of his cheap, mediciney cologne. I heard him yelling, "You're gonna feel it! You're gonna feel it!" and I could feel his scraggly, teenaged beard against my cheek.

I turned over so quickly Paula almost fell off the bed.

"What's wrong?" she asked, alarmed.

I was breathing heavily, like I was having an asthma attack.

"Nothing," I said. "I just got a bad cramp in my leg."

"You scared me."

"I'm fine," I said. "Just give me a second."

Paula was quiet as I tried to catch my breath.

"Okay," I finally said. "I think I'm all right now."

"Does your leg still hurt?"

"No, it was just a cramp – probably from driving."

"You sure you're all right?"

"Where were we?"

We continued our foreplay. Then Paula tried to climb on top, but I pushed her aside again.

"Sorry," I said. "I think I might be coming down with something. You think we could –"

"It's okay," she said. "It's late anyway."

It was quiet in the room except for wind rattling the windowpanes. I was starting to doze, but Paula was still wide awake, running her fingers through my sweaty chest hair.

We had breakfast at the inn's restaurant. The atmosphere wasn't any more active or less depressing than it had been last night. There were a few couples at the other tables, but they were all in their seventies and eighties and I felt like I was in the cafeteria at a nursing home. I wanted to make a joke about it to Paula, but I knew she would get upset and accuse me of "trying to ruin the weekend." So I kept my mouth shut and instead made a few phony comments about how "peaceful" and "relaxing" it was up here in the off-season, and Paula smiled, agreeing, although I think she probably felt the same way I did.

After breakfast, we took a walk in town. "Town" was several quaint streets with small, artsy stores. It was a sunny, windy, chilly day. Most of the shops were open, but the streets were mainly empty and bleak. Paula seemed to be enjoying herself though, browsing in crafts stores. I was bored and sat down on a bench and read *The New York Times*. Later, at about ten-thirty, we decided we would go back to the room to change for tennis.

There were two courts at the end of town on Main Street. It was warming up outside, but it was still cool in the shade. Both courts were taken so Paula and I waited behind the gate.

Finally, the two older men who were playing on the court nearest to us finished their match and Paula and I went on.

I was out of shape and it showed. My timing and footwork were off and I couldn't get my backhand going. Paula was having difficulty covering the court too, but she was playing a lot better than I was.

"Excuse me!"

I looked over to my left and there was a guy, about my age, with wavy brown hair, standing alongside an attractive, dark-haired woman who looked like she was about twenty.

"Do you think we can hit with you for a while?" the man asked.

I thought this was pretty ballsy of him, especially since Paula and I had been on the court only for a few minutes. But then, remembering seeing a sign on the fence that the courts were for "Stockbridge town residents" only, I said, "Sure, I don't see why not."

The couple came onto the court and greeted us at the net. Their names were Doug and Kirsten. Paula and I introduced ourselves and we all shook hands. Kirsten had a very small head. She was pretty, but vacuous-looking. Doug was about my height, but he was in great shape with thin, toned legs and cut muscles. They both sounded like they were from New York – definitely not locals – and I already regretted inviting them to play with us. Doug was wearing an expensive tennis outfit – a short-sleeved sweater and matching shorts – and Kirsten was wearing a clean white tennis dress. They each had brought three rackets and Doug had a large gym bag stuffed with God knows what.

I looked at Paula, rolling my eyes, but she didn't seem to understand what I thought was so funny.

The four of us started hitting and I knew right away that this wasn't going to be fun. Doug and Kirsten had good strokes, but they were taking themselves much too seriously. The way he grunted and she squealed after each shot, it sounded like they were having loud sex.

After rallying for about ten minutes, Doug said, "So are you guys ready for a match?"

"I don't think so," I said.

"Why not?" Paula asked me.

"I don't know," I said. "I mean, if everybody else wants to play I guess I'm game."

Doug came to the net and wanted to spin his racket to decide who served first, but I said, "It's all right. You guys can serve."

"Then you choose the side."

"This side is fine," I said.

"Okay, if you don't want the wind. Whose balls should we use?"

"We can use mine."

"When did you open them?"

"Today."

He examined one of the balls suspiciously. "They're Spalding and we prefer Wilson. Do you mind if we use our balls?"

"Be my guest," I said.

Doug served the first game. After double faulting, he shouted "Fuck!" and when Kirsten missed a volley at the net during the next point he yelled, "Come on!" I thought of the old saying, how a person's true personality comes out on the tennis court. If this was true, Doug was the world's biggest jerk.

After we won the first three games, Doug became increasingly nasty. He kept cursing at himself and at Kirsten and when I called one of his balls out he gave me a long, John McEnroe-like stare. I was afraid he was going to start throwing his racket.

Meanwhile, Paula and I were getting winded, breathing hard after every point, and Doug and Kirsten won the next few games. Now that they were playing better, Doug stopped yelling, but he was just as fiercely competitive. After I hit a weak return of serve, he hit an overhead that just missed Paula's head. He said he was sorry, but I knew he was aiming for her.

We wound up losing the set. I was willing to call it a match right there, but they wanted to play best two out of three and, for some reason, so did Paula.

At this point, I couldn't care less who won, but now Paula was taking the match as seriously as our opponents, as if Doug's cut-throat personality had rubbed off on her. When I missed a backhand on a ball hit to the center of the court, she said seriously, "From now on let those balls go."

"But it was on my side of the court," I said.

"It doesn't matter – let me take them. My forehand is a lot better than your backhand."

If we were alone, I wouldn't have let a comment like that go, but I didn't want to get into a big shouting match around strangers.

We wound up losing the second set and the match. Victorious, Doug's personality changed. He greeted us, smiling, at the net.

"Great game, guys," he said.

I was ready to shake hands and leave, but Paula wanted to stick around and have a conversation. It turned out that Doug and Kirsten were boyfriend and girlfriend, and that they lived in separate apartments in Manhattan, on the Upper East Side, not far from Paula and me. It also turned out that they were staying at the Red Lion Inn this weekend. It annoyed me that we suddenly had so much in common.

"It's a nice place," Doug said in regard to the inn, "but looks like the geriatric crowd's up here this weekend, huh?"

Paula laughed, although I knew if I made a crack like that she wouldn't have thought it was funny.

Kirsten was smiling with her perfect white teeth.

Doug talked for a while about the Berkshires versus the Hamptons and how much better the Hamptons were. Then he said, "I have an idea – if you guys don't have any plans tonight, how about you join us for dinner?"

Before I could make up an excuse, Paula said, "That sounds great."

Doug suggested that we meet on the front porch of the inn at seven o'clock, then he and Kirsten continued to play tennis, grunting and squealing.

Walking away next to Paula, I decided not to say anything. I was so angry I knew that it would be impossible to have a normal conversation and that I was better off waiting until I cooled down. But Paula never let anything go and, after about a minute or two of silence, she said, "So why are you so mad at me?"

"Forget it," I said.

"I don't get it," she said. "You didn't want to have dinner with them tonight?"

"No, I'd love to have dinner with them. Tennis was so much fun, dinner should be a blast."

"If you didn't want to go you should have said something."

"Maybe if you gave me the chance –"

"I can't tell what you want to do. I'm not a fucking mind reader."

"Asking me might've helped."

"What's so bad about having dinner with them?"

"They're annoying."

"I don't think they're so annoying."

"Well, I do. Besides, I thought the point was to spend a weekend alone."

"It's just dinner."

"And what was with your attitude before?"

"My *attitude*?"

"You were getting so competitive."

"We were playing a game."

"Exactly – a game."

"The object of a game is to win."

"No, the object of a game is to have fun."

"It's possible to win *and* have fun."

"You didn't seem to be having much fun."

"*Me?*"

"Miss My-Forehand-Is-a-Lot-Better-Than-Your-Backhand."

"So I got competitive. It's better than being lazy."

When we got back to the room I locked myself in the bathroom and took a long shower. Knowing that Paula was sweaty and anxious to wash up, I took my sweet time.

I knew what Paula had *really* meant was that I was lazy with my career, that I wasn't ambitious enough. She had hit me with similar put-downs over the years, ever since she had gotten her MBA. She used to encourage me to go back to school all the time, casually mentioning the husbands of friends of hers who had just completed law school or gotten their MBAs – hint, hint! Her passive-aggressiveness cooled while I was raking in the big bucks at my last job, but now that she was a vice president and I was fighting to keep my sales career alive she was starting to get her digs in again.

Finally, I came out of the bathroom with a towel around my waist. Paula was lying in bed, watching a movie on TV.

For a few minutes, while I was getting dressed, we didn't speak. Then Paula said, "I'm sorry. You're right – I shouldn't've snapped at you."

"It's my fault," I said, tired of being angry at her. "I was making a big deal about nothing."

"If you really don't feel like having dinner with them tonight of course we can cancel. You know I'd rather eat alone with you – I just didn't want to be rude."

"It's all right," I said. "Maybe I just had a bad first impression of them. Maybe they're not so bad."

After Paula showered and got dressed, we took a drive up Route 7 to Lenox. The small New Englandy town catered to the Tanglewood Music Festival, which wouldn't open for another couple of months, so it was even quieter and more deserted than Stockbridge.

I didn't want to complain to Paula, but so far this weekend had been depressing and not very relaxing and I wished we had just stayed in the city.

Back in the room, I napped while Paula watched TV. I slept in an awkward position and woke up with neck pain and a headache. I took a couple of Tylenols, which helped the pain, but I was still groggy and in a generally lousy mood. Paula got surprisingly dressed up for dinner, wearing a black cut-velvet dress she had bought a few weeks ago for four hundred dollars at a boutique on Madison Avenue. I put on a pair of chinos and a black button-down shirt from Banana Republic.

At seven o'clock, we arrived in the lobby and saw Doug and Kirsten waiting near the main entrance. They were decked out. Kirsten looked like she had stepped out of *Vogue*, in a long brown dress with two- or three-inch heels, and Doug was Mr *GQ* in a beige linen sport jacket and a white linen shirt and beige slacks. We exchanged hellos, then walked in the cool night to the restaurant. Doug was talking about tennis – how he had been playing since he was five years old and how he was once a ranked amateur player in New Jersey. I zoned out, still trying to get out of my bad mood. The sun was setting and the wind had died down.

The restaurant was small, but surprisingly active. There were about six or seven tables and they were all filled. Doug had made a reservation, so we were seated ahead of the two couples waiting at the door.

Doug worked on Wall Street and he and Paula started a discussion about the stock market. Paula mentioned some stock her company was researching and Doug chimed in with comments about "p.e. ratios," "hedge funds," and "the Asian markets." Judging by their intensity and enthusiasm, I think they both forgot that Kirsten and I were sitting at the table. Finally, I struck up a dull conversation with Kirsten. My initial impression of her was dead-on – beyond her pretty smile there wasn't much there. She worked as an executive assistant at an ad agency and it seemed as if her responses to anything I said were either "really," "wow," or "no way." She seemed like she would be an easy person to get along with, though – definitely not as headstrong as Paula. It made sense that Doug would be attracted to her, since he seemed like the type of guy who had zero tolerance for opinions that differed from his own.

"So what do you do, Robert?" Doug asked, as if noticing me for the first time.

"It's Richard," I said.

"Richard, right. Sorry, must've gotten a little heatstroke on the tennis court today."

Paula laughed.

"I sell computer networking services," I said.

"Oh, a techie," Doug said. "Hey, maybe you could swing by my room later and fix my laptop. I can't seem to get my modem to work."

"I'm not a computer *technician*," I said. "I sell networking systems."

Paula gave me a nasty look.

"Oh, I get it," Doug said. "So you must go out of town a lot, huh? Leave your wife all alone."

"No, most of my business is in the city," I said.

"Oh, well, that's good," Doug said. "Of course, at my job I have to travel a lot – meet with division heads all over the world. I just came back from Singapore last week."

"I've always wanted to go to Singapore," Paula said excitedly.

Doug went on, in his loud, grating voice, trying to impress us all with his world travels. Meanwhile, I couldn't stop noticing the way he was flirting with Paula. He wouldn't take his eyes off her and he was sitting closer to her than he was to Kirsten.

I watched as Paula seemed to be having the time of her life, drinking wine, laughing at every dumb wisecrack Doug made. Not wanting to get back into the alcohol habit, I was drinking iced tea. I hoped that no one would want to order dessert or coffee so we could get out of the restaurant as soon as possible.

Then I snapped out of my stupor when Doug said, "So are you two planning to start a family soon?"

"In a year or two," I said.

"No kidding?!" Drinking was making Doug even louder and more boisterous. "So are you going to stay in the city or move to the suburbs?"

"Move to the suburbs," I said. "That is, if we can ever find a way to unload our apartment."

"That sounds like a great plan," Doug said. "I grew up in northwest Jersey, in a house with a big backyard and a tennis court. I don't think a kid should have it any other way."

The waiter came and asked if we wanted dessert. At first, everyone said no – thank God – then Doug said, "I can't resist – I'll have the *tiramisù*."

The waiter left and I looked over and saw Paula glaring at me. It was only a quick glance, but I could tell she was furious. I had no idea why. The only reason I could think of was that it had something to do with dessert. Maybe she'd seen me make a face.

For the rest of the meal, I knew Paula was still fuming, but I doubted Doug and Kirsten realized anything was wrong. Finally, the check arrived. Doug suggested we split it down the middle, even though he'd had the most expensive entrée, drunk the most wine, and was the only one to order dessert.

Walking back to the inn, Doug said, "You know, there's a little nightclub in the hotel, in the basement. I don't think it's gonna exactly be like the China Club down there, but there's supposed to be live music. I guess that's opposed to dead music." He laughed. "Anyway, it's probably the most exciting thing to do up here at night."

I was about to say no thank you, but Paula beat me to it.

"I'm sorry," she said, "but I'm not feeling too well."

"Oh no," Kirsten said. "Was it something you ate?"

"I don't know," Paula said. "Maybe."

"Are you all right?" Doug said, overly concerned, as if he were Paula's father.

"I'm fine," Paula said. "I just want to go back to the room and rest."

In front of the inn, Paula and I said goodnight and then we headed through the lobby.

"What's wrong?" I said.

"Just leave me the fuck alone," she said.

Jesus, here we go again.

"You know, I'm really getting sick of this shit," I said.

"I really don't care what you're getting sick of."

"Every two minutes getting pissed off at me, having these ridiculous fights."

We walked upstairs in silence. On the second floor, Paula said, "I'm going to sleep."

"I wish you would tell me what I did wrong."

When we were inside the room, Paula said, "Don't you think we should discuss if or when we're having children before you start making public announcements?"

"What are you talking about?" I said. "You always said you wanted kids before you were thirty-five."

"And when was the last time we discussed that?" she said, glaring at me.

"Jesus, why do you have to pick fights about every little thing?"

"Having a family isn't 'little'! I haven't heard you say a word about children since... I don't know when. Then, all of a sudden, it's all decided – we're having kids 'in a year or two.'"

"I thought that was the plan."

"Whose plan? There's a lot up in the air right now. You don't know what's happening with your job, I just got a new job. I'm not ready to stay home and raise a family. And I definitely don't want to move out of the city to a house in the suburbs – where the hell did you get that idea?"

Paula walked away into the bathroom and I followed her.

"I hope you're not serious about any of this," I said.

"I'm very serious," she said. "I've been talking about all of this with Dr Carmadie. I'm not sure what I want yet."

"And you say I'm the one who doesn't discuss things? You'll talk about kids with your fucking therapist, but you won't talk to me!"

I felt like I was losing control, that if this went on any further I'd start saying things I'd regret.

"We can discuss it right now if you want to," she said.

"You know what I think?" I said. "I think this has nothing to do with whether you want kids or not. I think it has to do with me. You're not sure you want *my* kids."

"Oh, really –"

"Maybe I'm too lazy for you," I said. "Maybe you want some arrogant hotshot Wall Street guy like Doug."

"*What?*"

"I saw the way you were flirting with him, laughing at every fucking word that came out of his mouth, like he was Robin Fucking Williams. See, I'm right – your face is turning red. You were flirting with him, weren't you?"

"Will you shut the hell up?"

"Why don't you go downstairs and find him – I'm sure Kirsten won't mind. They're probably swingers – maybe the two of you could fuck him at the same time."

Paula had been looking away. Now she turned back toward me and screamed, "Get out of here, you bastard! Get the hell out!"

I stormed out of the room, slamming the door, and took the stairs down to the lobby. I walked toward the tennis courts then, realizing I was cold, I turned around and headed back toward the inn.

Still too upset to go back to the room, I sat on the porch, in one of the rocking chairs facing Main Street. There were two young women on the porch a few yards away from me. They looked like they were in their mid-twenties. One of the girls had long, curly brown hair; the other one had short red hair. They looked bored and very single. They had probably come up here for the weekend from Boston or New York, hoping to meet guys. The dark-haired girl looked over at me. I imagined starting a conversation with her, secretly sliding my wedding ring off and putting it in my pocket, then going back to her room.

Making sure my hand with my wedding band was concealed, I smiled at the dark-haired girl. She seemed surprised, maybe slightly disgusted, and turned back to her friend. A few seconds later, they got up and left.

In the morning Paula and I pretended our fight last night had never happened. We had a nice breakfast at the inn and then we spent the day together, driving around the nearby towns, without arguing at all.

In the afternoon, we headed back to the city, along the winding upstate New York roads. Paula fell asleep, leaning against the door, and I was relaxing, listening to *The Prairie Home Companion* on National Public Radio, when I saw myself standing outside my old house in Brooklyn, bouncing a basketball. Michael Rudnick came over from across the street and said, "Hey, Richie, wanna play some Ping-Pong?"

"Sure!" I said.

I put my basketball down on the lawn and followed Rudnick to his house.

"So you think you can beat me this time?" he asked.

"Yeah," I said.

"We'll see about that," he said.

We went up the driveway and entered the house through the back door. It was dark and very quiet. Rudnick told me to go down to the basement ahead of him and I heard the door close behind us.

We were playing Ping-Pong. The score was 20–14, Rudnick leading. Rudnick served and my return hit the net. Rudnick put down his paddle and started chasing me from behind.

"You're gonna feel it! You're gonna feel it!"

I was running away, laughing. Rudnick grabbed me from behind and started yanking on my underwear.

"You're gonna feel it! You're gonna feel it!"

I was lying facedown on the couch and Rudnick was on top of me, grunting and sweating. I wasn't laughing anymore. I was trying to get away, but he was too strong for me.

"Please stop," I begged him. "Please stop."

I tried to break away, using my arm for leverage, when I realized I wasn't in the basement anymore, I was in the car, yanking on the steering wheel. The car had swerved off the shoulder, onto a grassy area, and there was a tree straight ahead. I braked and turned the steering wheel far to the left. Paula woke up screaming. The car missed the tree by a few yards as we skidded back onto the highway. Luckily, there wasn't another car coming or we would have been in a serious accident.

"It's okay, sweetie," I said, feeling light-headed and slightly in shock. "Don't worry – it's okay, it's okay."

"What happened?"

"I don't know. I think a raccoon ran onto the road."

"A raccoon?"

"It doesn't matter. It's over."

We drove on. Paula stayed wide awake and neither of us said a word.

5

Monday morning Paula and I shared a cab downtown. I got out at Forty-eighth Street, kissing her goodbye quickly, and then she continued to Wall Street.

As always after spending an entire weekend together, it felt strange to be alone. I also felt guilty about the way I'd been treating Paula lately. Not only was she my wife, she was my best friend, maybe my only friend, and I realized how empty my life would be without her.

I used to have a lot of friends, but over the years most of them had gotten married or moved away and I hardly saw them anymore. At my jobs, I'd always had acquaintances, but no one I wanted to get together with outside the office. My two room-mates from college still lived in the city – Joe on the West Side and Stu in the Village. But Joe was married now and he and his wife were high school teachers and I didn't have a lot in common with them. Stu was a web designer and we always had a lot to talk about, but he was single and didn't have a steady girlfriend to double-date with, so we rarely got together.

I didn't have much family, either. My mother lived in Austin, Texas, with her second husband. She had become more and more religious over the years and we weren't very close. My father lived in Southern California with his wife, but he was a selfish prick and I spoke to him as little as possible. I had a couple of aunts and uncles and cousins, but they lived outside New York and we didn't keep in touch.

At my office, I decided to call my mother, just to say hi. I hadn't spoken to her in a while, at least a month, and I thought it would be nice to talk to someone from my family.

"Richie, what a pleasant surprise," my mother said,

although I could tell she didn't sound exactly excited to hear from me. Every time I spoke with my mother lately I became very agitated and annoyed, and I was already regretting that I'd called her.

"So how's everything in New York?" my mother asked. "How's Paula?"

"New York's fine, Paula's great."

"Well, I'm very glad to hear that. So why are you calling?"

"I'm just calling to say hi," I said.

"Oh. Well, that's nice. It's always nice to hear from you, Richie. How's the weather in New York?"

"The weather here's great," I said, upset that my relationship with my mother had become so shallow. "How's the weather in Texas?"

"Hot as usual. We've also had a lot of rain lately. Yesterday, Charlie and I had to walk to church in the pouring rain. Have you and Paula been going to church lately?"

"No, we haven't," I said, bracing for an attack.

"Richie, what's wrong with you? You have to go to church. Don't you want to have a relationship with God?"

"We just haven't had a lot of time lately –"

"You don't have time for God? Don't tell me you haven't been going to confession, either?"

"Can't we please talk about something else?"

"You have to go to confession, Richie. Doesn't Paula go to confession?"

"Ma, please," I said, raising my voice.

"Richie, I'm very disappointed in you."

"So is anything new with you?" I asked.

"I know what your problem is," my mother said, "it's Paula. She's a bad influence on you. I'll never understand why you married a Protestant. Couldn't you find a nice Catholic girl to marry?"

"Whoops, I have a call coming in on the other line," I said, making an excuse to get off the phone. "Yep, just heard the beep again. It was really nice talking to you, Ma. I'll call again soon."

"Go to church," my mother said. "God is waiting for you."

I hung up and called Paula at work.

"Hi, honey," I said. "I just wanted to tell you how much I love you and I miss you very much."

There was a long pause – I could tell she was surprised and confused – then she said, "I love you, too."

"That's all I wanted to say," I said. "'Bye, sweetie."

Over the weekend, I'd somehow managed to forget all about work. It was depressing to suddenly remember that I was in the midst of a miserable sales slump and that my job was on the line. I had logged on to the internet, doing some price researching for my eleven o'clock sales meeting, when Steve Ferguson poked his head into my office.

"Hope I'm not interrupting anything," he said with his usual slick smile. He looked tanner than he did on Friday. He always had a tan, even in the middle of winter – he either went to salons or had tanning cream professionally applied – but today he looked especially bronze.

"No, just getting ready for a meeting," I said.

"Actually, that's what I'm here about," Steve said, entering my office. "Bob suggested that I sit in on the meeting with you – see if I can give you some pointers."

"That's all right," I said.

"Actually," Steve said, "Bob didn't suggest it – he *told* me to come with you. If you have a problem with it, you can talk to him, but I'd be happy to help out."

"Whatever," I said.

"Great. Just come by my office to pick me up when you're ready to rock and roll."

This was all I needed – if I didn't have enough hints that my head was on the chopping block, now Bob was sending Steve to baby-sit me in a sales meeting.

The appointment was with Jim Turner, the MIS manager at Loomis & Caldwell, a midsized ad agency on Sixth Avenue. They were converting their system from Windows NT to Linux with a nice chunk of hardware and consulting involved, and the company had potential to turn into a six-figure client. My phone conversation with Jim had gone great and he was very eager to meet with me.

The Loomis & Caldwell office was only a few blocks away so Steve and I walked there. Steve was going on and on about cars and vacation spots and I tried to pay as little attention as possible.

The secretary said that Jim Turner would see us right away – a good sign, because it was about fifteen minutes before the scheduled time for the meeting. It was the first time I'd met Jim in person and I got good vibes from our handshake. I introduced Steve as "a colleague of mine," then I went right into my pitch. It couldn't have gone better. Jim said he was extremely unhappy with his current consulting company and that he was eager to start a new relationship. He was impressed with our client list and credentials and he wanted to start talking specifics. Then Steve cut in. With his usual used-car-salesman persona, talking fast out of the side of his mouth, he bragged about how our company was the "best" consulting firm in the city and how our clients were always "one-hundred-and-ten-percent" satisfied. I could tell that Jim was put off by Steve's grating personality, that he was the type of client who didn't need to be sold, who was going to make up his own mind. But Steve had no clue what was going on. A few times, I wanted to yell "Shut up!" or, better yet, tackle him to the floor and beat him senseless. But I just sat there, watching Jim check his watch and grind his teeth, obviously trying to restrain his own frustration.

Finally, Steve shut up. I took over, trying to go over some specifics, but Jim suggested that I just take the request-for-proposal back to the office and send him a bid. Obviously, Steve's monologue had killed the deal. Jim had said that one of his major gripes about his current consulting firm was that they were "too pushy," and Steve's personality had definitely raised a red flag.

Jim walked us out to the lobby. His goodbye handshake was much weaker than his hello handshake, and although he insisted that he was "eager" to see our quote, I knew this was just polite bullshit; there was no way in hell he was going to use our services.

Waiting for the elevator with Steve, I was fuming. The receptionist was within earshot so I figured I'd wait until we were alone to say something. But as soon as the elevator doors closed, Steve beat me to it, saying, "Can I give you some constructive criticism?"

"*You* want to give *me* criticism?"

"Yeah, I noticed you didn't discuss pricing right away. Next time you might want to –"

"Will you just shut the fuck up?"

Steve stared at me. Then he said, "What the hell's the matter with you?"

"You totally fucked up the sale, you stupid asshole, that's what's the matter with me. He was interested, he wanted to talk specifics, but you had to open your big fat mouth."

"Hey, I think you should watch the way –"

"Fuck you."

"I was just doing what Bob *told* me to do. I was supposed to demonstrate how I close business –"

"No, you were supposed to sit in on the meeting – not take over the meeting. I know how to close sales. I'm a thousand-times-better closer than you'll ever be and I don't need an idiot like you fucking my shit up."

The elevator opened at the lobby and I stormed away. Not until I was out on Sixth Avenue did I realize exactly what I had just done, but I wasn't going to go back to apologize. The guy was a big-time jerk and I didn't regret anything I'd said to him. But I knew that the situation had the potential to lead to major trouble. Steve was the teacher's-pet type who was probably on his way to tattle on me to Bob Goldstein right now. Steve's secret agenda all along had probably been to get me canned. Right now, as part of a company policy to avoid having multiple salesmen call the same prospects, my leads were off-limits to him. But if I left the company, my leads would be fair game and he'd be able to take advantage of all the legwork I'd already done and make a few easy sales.

I looked at my watch and saw it was twenty to twelve. I went to the deli on Forty-eighth Street where I sometimes had lunch, but when I got there I decided I wasn't very hungry. Instead, I walked farther east, toward Madison Avenue.

I remembered the address for Michael J. Rudnick, Esquire, that I had gotten off the internet last week and I decided to go to the office building to see if this was the Michael Rudnick I knew. I had no idea what this would accomplish, but I wanted to see him again anyway.

It was still before twelve, so my idea was to hang out in front of his building on Fifty-fourth and Madison until one. I hoped he would leave the building for lunch before then. If not, I'd just come back some other time.

Probably because of the sunny, pleasant weather, there was a steady stream of people entering and leaving the building. I bought a knish from a cart on the corner, looking over my shoulder to make sure I didn't miss Rudnick. I returned to the building and ate the knish standing up, leaning against a ledge. There was a courtyard across from me with tables and chairs set up and people were seated, talking and eating. Along the adjacent building there was an artificial waterfall and a fountain at the bottom. After I finished the knish, I took off my suit jacket and mopped the sweat off my forehead with a napkin, still staring at the building.

I decided that I might be wasting my time. Even if Michael J. Rudnick, Esquire, was the right Michael Rudnick, how did I know he went out for lunch instead of eating in, or that he'd leave the building through the Fifty-fourth Street exit? Maybe there was another exit on Madison Avenue or on Fifty-fifth Street.

It was almost one o'clock and there was still no sign of him. I decided to wait ten more minutes. When the ten minutes passed, I decided to wait another five. Finally, I gave up. Walking back toward Madison, I called my office on my cellphone to see if I had any messages – I didn't. I put the phone away in my briefcase when Rudnick appeared, walking toward me. He was with another man, and they were both smiling and laughing. Unlike the other day, Michael wasn't wearing sunglasses, and now I was absolutely positive that it was him. His eyebrows were the clincher. He had plucked the hairs above his nose to eliminate the caterpillar effect, but each eyebrow was just as thick and noticeable as when he was a teenager.

He was about ten yards away when I first spotted him, but it seemed to take forever until we passed. I was aware of how terrified I felt, like a kid in a classroom when he's called on unexpectedly by a teacher. My back was sweating and I was even starting to shake. When Michael was a few feet in front of me, his gaze shifted and he was staring right at me. Suddenly, he stopped smiling. He was probably only looking at me for an instant, but it seemed much longer, and his narrow, dark eyes were like lasers. Even though I was taller than he was and I probably weighed at least twenty pounds more than he did, I felt like he was ten feet tall, with Mike Tyson's body, and I was an anorexic midget. I didn't feel like an adult anymore either. I was just a weak, naive, defenseless ten-year-old.

As Rudnick passed by I heard him say, in a surprisingly

deep voice, "Could be." After a few seconds, I turned around to see if he was looking back at me. He wasn't. Either he hadn't recognized me or he had ignored me on purpose. I watched him approach the office building on Madison and Fifty-fourth Street and enter through the revolving doors.

Back at my office, I was still feeling shaken up and a little dazed when Heidi rang and said that Bob wanted to see me right away. When I asked what about, she said, "He just wants to see you."

I knew it – Steve, that son of a bitch, must have ratted on me already. Definitely not in the mood to deal with this crap now, I went to the men's room and splashed my face with cold water. I wiped my face with a paper towel, adjusted my tie while looking in the mirror above the sink, then went to meet with Bob.

Bob was standing, staring at a sheet of paper, when I arrived at his office. The sleeves of his white dress shirt were rolled up to his elbows, and his black yarmulke was on slightly crooked.

"Richard," he said without emotion. "Take a seat."

I sat down and then he sat down across from me, at his desk.

"I know what this is all about," I said. "Steve probably talked to you, but I can explain –"

"I don't want any explanations," Bob said. There was a serious tone in his voice that I had never heard before. "First of all, where have you been for the past forty-five minutes?"

"Lunch," I said.

"Steve said your meeting this morning let out at eleven thirty." He looked at his watch. "It's after one-thirty now."

"The meeting let out later than eleven-thirty," I said.

"All employees at this company are allowed one hour for lunch," Bob said. "It's in the contract you signed when you started working here. Normally, I wouldn't be a hard-ass about this. If it happened one time, I wouldn't say anything, but now that it seems to be turning into a habit –"

"A habit? When did I ever take a long lunch?"

"What time did you leave on Friday?"

"I don't remember."

"Our computer records show you swiped out at three-thirty. Again, ordinarily I wouldn't be checking up on you, but I just don't understand what you think you're doing. You're not producing and then you're taking all of these liberties."

"I left early one day," I said, "because I had to pick up a rental car. I usually arrive early and leave late and most days I don't even take lunch."

"The other thing I wanted to talk to you about," Bob said, changing the subject, "is what happened at your sales meeting this morning."

"Steve screwed up an easy sale for me, that's what happened."

"He said he was trying to help you and then you started screaming at him in the elevator."

"That isn't what happened –"

"To tell you the truth, I don't care what happened, all right? I can sit here all day listening to you two point fingers at each other and it won't accomplish anything. I'm only concerned with one thing – the bottom line – and the fact is, Steve's the top producer at this company and you haven't closed any business so far. Until that changes I think you should watch what you say and to whom you say it. Right now I don't think you're in a position to say he 'screwed up' anything for you."

"You weren't there."

"I mean it," Bob said. "You're a nice guy. I like you, and I think you can make a lot of money for this company. But you have to start showing some respect for your fellow employees and this job or you're not going to last here. I'm sorry, but that's just the way it is. Is this understood?"

"Yes," I said humbly.

"Good. There's one more thing I need to discuss with you. It has to do with the office situation. You're going to have to move out into a cubicle. It's only temporary – we'll move you back into an office as soon as the space develops – but for right now you'll have to move."

"Is this because I'm not producing?"

"No, it has nothing to do with that. It just has to do with seniority. Since you're newer to the company I think you should be the one to move. I know it's not the best solution in the world, but it'll have to do for now."

I wanted to quit on the spot, but I also felt like I had something to prove. If I quit it would be like admitting that Steve was a better salesman than I was.

For the rest of the afternoon, I tried to make *something* happen on the phone, but I was too distracted. I kept thinking about Michael Rudnick. Just remembering the way he was smiling, looking so happy, upset the hell out of me. I made a few token calls, then I spent the rest of the afternoon surfing the web.

I made sure I didn't leave work until a few minutes *after* five. Leaving my office building, I felt the way I used to feel when school was let out – instantly free, thrilled that I didn't have to return to the hellhole until tomorrow.

On my way home, I decided to stop at the Old Stand on Fifty-fifth and Third for a quick drink. The Old Stand was an Irish bar, and it was filled with the after-work crowd – mostly rowdy young guys in shirts and ties. I ordered a rum and Coke and drank it in several gulps. I was about to order a refill when I realized what I was doing. I knew I could *handle* another drink – I wasn't an alcoholic, for Christ's sake – but I didn't want to have to come home slightly drunk and have Paula start yelling at me. So even though I really wanted another drink, and could have used one, I left the bar.

It was a sunny, pleasant late afternoon. I still had a lot on my mind, but the buzz from the alcohol made my problems seem much less important.

I arrived at my apartment before six o'clock. After I walked Otis, I sat on the couch in my underwear, watching TV.

Around six-thirty, Paula came home. Holding her pumps, with Otis trailing her, she entered the living room and kissed me hello. Neither of us was in the mood to go shopping or cook so we ordered from an Italian place on First Avenue – chicken parm for me and grilled portobello mushrooms and a spinach salad for Paula. We were having a casual conversation about work – Paula talked about how much she liked her new job and that she was going to be moving into a bigger office. Although I felt a strong pang of jealousy I think I hid my emotions well. I told her how proud I was of her and that her company was lucky to have someone like her working for them. When she asked me how things were going at my job I said, "Great," and told her that my meeting today had gone "very smoothly."

We had finished eating and we were cleaning off the table, putting the empty containers into a plastic shopping bag, when Paula said casually, "Oh, I forgot to tell you – Doug called me today."

For a couple of seconds I was confused – maybe I was thinking about other things. Then I said, "Doug? You mean Doug-from-the-Berkshires Doug?"

"Yeah, I told him where I worked the other night, so he looked me up. He said he was sorry we left without having a chance to say goodbye."

"But why did he call you?"

"That was it. And to ask if we want to get together sometime."

"The two of you get together?"

"No, the four of us."

"What did you tell him?"

"I said okay, but we don't *have* to go. I knew you wouldn't be thrilled about it. He gave me his number, so the ball's in our court."

"I don't want to go."

"I knew that's how you'd feel. It's fine with me. I really don't care one way or the other."

We finished clearing off the table, then we sat in the living room together and watched TV. I didn't like the idea of Doug calling Paula at work – who the hell did that guy think he was, calling my wife? – but I didn't want to say anything to her about it. After all the arguing this weekend I wanted to have a peaceful, relaxing evening at home.

At around nine-thirty I put my hand on Paula's lap and asked her if she wanted to go to bed early.

"Okay," she said.

I walked Otis. When I returned Paula was in the bathroom throwing up.

"Are you all right?" I asked outside the door.

"Yes," she said, sounding awful. "Maybe it was the mushrooms, or something in my salad."

She stayed in the bathroom for about another ten minutes, occasionally vomiting, then she got into bed with me, looking pale.

"You don't look too good," I said. "Maybe you should drink some water."

"I'm all right," she said. "I just need to go to sleep."

I knew that Paula was telling the truth, that she *did* need rest, but I couldn't help feeling slightly rejected. Last night we'd been tired from traveling and gone straight to bed, so we hadn't made love since Thursday night. Ordinarily, this wouldn't have bothered me. We had gone through long dry spells before and it was never a big deal. But now

I couldn't help wondering if Paula was just making up excuses.

Lying in bed next to her, I started reading one of my sales books, but I couldn't focus. An idea kept gnawing at me. At first, I thought it was probably just baseless paranoia, then I was convinced it was true.

This morning, in the cab, Paula had mentioned to me that her period was a couple of days late this month. At the time, I thought nothing of it – she said her breasts were sore and that she thought she had spotted a few days ago – but now she was vomiting and I couldn't help thinking she must be pregnant. Ordinarily, I would have been excited about this, but, remembering what she had said the other day about not wanting to give up her career for a child, I feared the worst. She *knew* she was pregnant this weekend, which was why she had prepared me in advance – letting me know that she didn't want a child *before* announcing that she was going to get an abortion. And there was only one logical explanation why she was suddenly so against children – the baby wasn't mine. She had been having an affair, after all, with Andy Connelly or with someone else. Maybe she'd been screwing someone from her office, or even her therapist, Dr Carmadie.

I was about to wake Paula up to confront her when I realized how crazy I was acting – ready to accuse my wife of cheating when she probably had a mild case of food poisoning.

I closed my eyes, trying to relax, when I was suddenly back in Michael Rudnick's basement. It was the same as last time except for one major difference. After I was underneath him on the couch for a while there was a voice from upstairs, "Michael!"

It was Michael's brother Kenneth, who was a couple of years younger than Michael and a few years older than me, calling down to the basement.

"I'll be right there!" Michael yelled, scrambling to put on his pants.

Then, remembering how Rudnick had been smiling so smugly on the way into his office building today, I became even more upset. I imagined cornering him in some back alley and beating him to death with a baseball bat. I was screaming, "Die, motherfucker, die!" as I swung the bat repeatedly against his head.

I couldn't fall asleep. Finally, I went into the living room, watching the news for a while, then I turned off the TV and went to the liquor cabinet. I poured myself half a glass of Scotch and then I went to the kitchen and mixed it with seltzer. After I finished the drink and replaced the glass, I went back to the liquor cabinet and checked the bottle to make sure Paula hadn't put any pen marks on the label.

6

When I entered my office, at around eight-thirty, the handymen were already constructing a cubicle for me adjacent to where the secretaries in the sales department worked. I was informed that I had to have everything out of my office within an hour so that they could start tearing down the walls.

I tried not to think about the situation. Instead, I told myself that this was only temporary – once the tide turned and I had some clout I'd either demand a new office or get a job at another company. Until then, I'd have to pretend this was all a bad dream.

I didn't have very much stuff to move. I put some files and books into a couple of boxes, but most of my information was on disk. I cleared out my desk and gathered some small objects – a coffee mug, a stapler, a paperweight. I wanted to get back to work right away, but I had to wait for the IT guys to hook up my computer and my phone line. In the meantime, I logged on to my laptop and sat in a corner doing some work, preparing for my eleven o'clock.

Finally, my new workstation was ready. I organized myself and got to work as quickly as possible. I was so embroiled in what I was doing I almost forgot that I was sitting in a cubicle, until Joe from Marketing came over to me and said, "This really sucks, man." Joe was a nice guy and I knew he meant well, but I still felt patronized. To everyone in the office I was a big joke now. They were probably whispering about me in the bathroom and by the water cooler: "Did you hear what happened to Richard Segal? He got kicked out of his office today." Jackie, a young secretary, passed by and said "Hi, Richard." When I had an office, she used to say "Hello, Richard." But now that I was a fellow cubicle worker she obviously felt comfortable and informal enough around me to say "Hi."

I left for my eleven o'clock meeting, glad to have the opportunity to get away from the office for a while. It turned out to be the best meeting I'd had in a long time. An insurance company on Church Street needed four Windows NT consultants with programming experience for an ongoing project and I really hit it off with Don Chaney, the MIS manager. He was a young guy, about thirty, and at the end of the meeting he said he was willing to give our company a try-out. They were having an emergency with their web server and he wanted to use one of our consultants to resolve it. Assuming the job went well, he would sign us up for the major project.

From Chaney's office, I called Jill in Recruiting at my company to see if we had a web consultant available for this afternoon. Jill said that Mark Singer, one of our top technicians, could be downtown by two o'clock. Chaney was thrilled. We shook hands and I told him I'd call him later in the day to see how the project was going.

Riding the subway uptown, I felt better about my job than I had in a long time. I had a big foot in the door with what could turn into a major contract. This could be the momentum swinger I'd been waiting for. Before I knew it, I'd be closing sales left and right and then I could go into Bob Goldstein's office and command some respect.

I didn't want to risk being caught for taking another long lunch, so when I got off the subway I picked up a corned beef on rye from a deli and took it to go.

Back at the office, I passed Steve Ferguson in the hallway. I was planning to say hello and perhaps apologize for the way I'd behaved yesterday, but he passed by me without looking at me or saying anything. I laughed to myself and shook my head. If he wanted to act like a child, that was up to him, and if he never spoke to me again it wouldn't exactly be a great loss.

I ate lunch in my cubicle while I prepared the quote for

the four consultants. My old confidence was back. I was the best goddamn computer-networking salesman in New York. Soon I'd have a corner office and my own secretary and my whole life would be different.

My phone rang. It was Jill from Recruiting and she said she needed to talk to me right away. I figured it had to do with the billing for Don Chaney's web server job. She probably wanted to know if I wanted to bill on a fixed rate or on an hourly basis. I finished the last bite of my sandwich, then I went down the hallway to Jill's office.

Jill was several years older than me, with an anorexic's body and short, curly brown hair. She had a very repressed, "corporate" personality. She rarely smiled, so I wasn't alarmed when I saw her serious, concerned expression.

"What's up?" I asked.

"I'm afraid I have some bad news for you about Mark Singer," Jill said. "He can't make it to your client site this afternoon."

Now I knew the situation *was* serious.

"What do you mean, *can't* make it?"

"I thought he was available, but an emergency came up at another site – with one of our current clients. I have no choice – I have to send him there."

"Isn't there somebody else you can send? This is extremely important."

She was shaking her head. "I'm sorry – all the other web server guys are busy. Can't you reschedule it for later in the week or early next week?"

"No," I said. I was starting to get very upset, losing control. "You know, you *told* me Mark would be available. I *told* my client he'd be there."

"He's not your client yet."

"What's this other company Mark has to go to?"

"What difference does it –"

"I want to know."

"Schaefer-Riley."

I knew it – one of Steve Fucking Ferguson's clients. The son of a bitch had probably manipulated all of this. He'd found out that I needed Mark today so he created an "emergency" at Schaefer-Riley, knowing a current client would get preference over a prospective one.

"This is bullshit," I said.

"Don't talk to me about it," she said, dismissing me. "If you have a problem, talk to Bob."

I stormed down the corridor to Bob's office. He was on the phone. He saw me standing there by his door and he looked over at me a few times, seeming annoyed. I didn't care. If I didn't get my way with this I was ready to quit, but *first* I was going to speak my mind.

Finally, Bob finished his call, "... All right, Joe. Thanks for taking the time to talk to me about this... 'Bye now." Then he hung up and said in an aggravated tone, "Can I help you with something?"

"Sorry to bother you," I said, "but it's an emergency."

"In the future, please don't barge into my office while I'm talking on the phone – I think I've spoken to you about that."

"I'm sorry," I said. "But I'm having a problem with Recruiting."

I explained the whole situation, then Bob said, "So what do you want me to do about it?"

"I was hoping you could talk to Steve," I said, "to find out if his project can be rescheduled."

"I'm not going to do that."

"Why not?"

"Because Steve is our top salesman right now and I respect his judgment."

"But, what I'm trying to explain, he doesn't really need my consultant for his client this afternoon. He's just doing this to screw me over because of what happened yesterday, and because he probably wants me out of here so he can take over my leads."

70

"I've made my decision," Bob said. "If there's nothing else you have to discuss with me, I'm extremely busy today."

I returned to my cubicle, ready to gather my things and quit. Then, gradually, my better sense returned. Quitting dramatically might give me some instant gratification, but I knew I'd regret it. It's much harder to find a new job when you're out of work, and I couldn't afford to go through a long period of unemployment. I'd be much better off staying at Midtown Consulting for as long as I could bear it and start sending out résumés and putting out some feelers to headhunters.

I called Don Chaney and explained that we wouldn't be able to fix his web server problem today. Predictably, he was disappointed. I asked him if he would still consider us for the larger project and he said, "Maybe. We'll see."

I knew I would never hear from him again.

I surfed the net awhile, trying to distract myself, then I called Paula. Her assistant said she was out to lunch with a friend and I said I'd try back later. I wondered what "friend" Paula could be having lunch with and I couldn't help imagining that she was with Doug. Maybe Doug had called her again at work and invited her out. Paula, caught off-guard, could have agreed, or maybe she didn't have to be coerced. I remembered how Doug had been hitting on her right in front of me in Stockbridge, and how Paula hadn't exactly seemed uninterested. It made sense that Doug would try to hit on Paula again in New York, and Paula could've easily been attracted to a guy who was better-looking than me and who was much more successful.

I called Paula on her cellphone. It rang three times, then she answered.

"Hi," I said. "What's going on?"

"Oh, hi," she said, uncomfortably.

"Did I get you at a bad time?"

"No... I mean not really. I was just having lunch."

"I know," I said. "I just called your office. Who are you having lunch with?"

She hesitated then said, "Debbie."

Debbie was a friend of Paula's from college with whom I'd thought Paula had fallen out of touch.

"Really?" I said. "Did you call her or did she call you?"

"I called her," Paula said. "I should really go now."

"Okay," I said. "Say hi to Debbie."

"I will. 'Bye."

Paula hung up. Even though I could picture the scene clearly – Doug sitting across from Paula, maybe holding her hand as she had an awkward conservation with me – I tried to stay calm, not jump to any conclusions.

I spent the rest of the afternoon working on my résumé and calling headhunters. One was confident that she'd find me something soon, but warned that the job market for high-end salespeople was "tight right now" and that I might have to "humble myself" and start at a "much lower salary" than I was currently making.

At 5:01, I left my office, feeling miserable. I went right across the street to a bar on Sixth Avenue. I weaved my way through the crowd of tourists from Kansas or wherever and found some room at the end of the bar. I ordered a Scotch and soda. The drink went too fast and it didn't relax me enough, so I ordered another. This one went as quickly as the first, so I bought a third. When I put the empty glass back on the bar I realized I was buzzed, maybe even drunk, and that I'd probably be very drunk once the alcohol made its way into my bloodstream. I was angry at myself for falling back into a bad habit so easily, but I also realized how my problems at work didn't seem nearly as important as they had about twenty minutes ago. Maybe if I had one more drink I'd feel even better. I waved the bartender over and ordered a refill. Number four went down as smoothly as the first three. I contemplated ordering a fifth, but I knew if I came home stumbling drunk it would lead to a big fight.

I decided to take a different route home for a change, through Central Park. I didn't realize how wrecked I was until I started bumping into people on Sixth Avenue.

The park was a surreal blur of joggers, trees, horses and buggies, and bicyclists. I walked unsteadily uptown along the park's East Drive. At one point I stumbled and a jogger, a young Asian woman, bumped into me and almost fell down.

"Moron!" she yelled, looking back over her shoulder.

Now I was extremely self-conscious. I knew how pathetic I must look – drunk, with my tie partially unwound and my hair a mess. I decided to rest for a while on a bench. I passed out quickly and woke up, groggy and disoriented. I checked my watch, surprised to see that it was 6:55. More than a half-hour had gone by in what seemed like an instant. I felt less drunk, but I was starting to experience hangover symptoms – a headache, dizziness, slight nausea. As I walked, I felt steadier and less disoriented. I was confident that, by the time I got home, Paula wouldn't be able to tell I'd been drinking.

I exited the park and headed east. I stopped at a deli on Madison and bought a medium-sized bottle of Evian. After chewing on a few Altoids, I took a sip of water, then I swished the liquid around in my mouth before swallowing. I drank the rest of the water in one long gulp, hoping to dilute the alcohol in my body, and then I continued home.

When I reached my building, I still wasn't sober, but I didn't think I looked drunk. I planned to tell Paula I wasn't feeling well and go right into the bedroom to lie down.

"Richard."

I was in the lobby, heading toward the elevators, when I turned and saw Paula, coming from the mailbox area.

She kissed me hello, then pulled back and stared at my face.

"What's wrong?" I asked, as if I were confused. The muscles in my face were weak and I felt like I didn't have complete control of my tongue.

"Have you been drinking?"

"No," I slurred. "I mean, I had a drink, yeah – with a client." I could tell she didn't believe me. A man arrived and the three of us got onto the same elevator. I hoped this "cooling-off period" would calm Paula down, but when we got off the elevator on the fifth floor she stage-whispered, "I can't believe you're drinking again."

"What?" I said, aware of how my entire face felt numb. "I told you I just had one. What's the big deal?"

She walked ahead of me, shaking her head, and opened the door to our apartment. Otis was barking and wagging his tail excitedly. Paula went directly to the bedroom and slammed the door. I was glad. I figured she'd stew alone for a while and then maybe I could convince her that she was getting upset at me for no reason.

I undressed in my office and put on a pair of shorts and a T-shirt that I found in a storage box of summer clothes. Then I went to the kitchen and took the restaurant menus out of the drawer and tried to decide what I was in the mood to eat for dinner.

"This time you're getting help."

Paula's voice startled me. I hadn't heard her leave the bedroom.

Looking back down at the menu from a Japanese restaurant, I said, "I'm not going to talk to you when you're acting crazy."

"I'm not going to go through this again."

"I told you – I had one drink with a client. I can have one fucking drink without you making a big deal about it."

"You're starting again – with the lies, the denial..."

I tried to step past her, to get to the phone, but she was blocking me.

74

"It can't just be all about work," she said. "It must have to do with me."

"You want sushi?" I asked.

She grabbed the receiver.

"Let go," I said.

"You're going to A.A."

"Let *go!* " I yanked harder and she released her grip.

"I wish you could see yourself right now," she said, her face turning pink. "It's like you're a different person. I don't know who you are anymore."

"Oh, stop with your fucking melodrama. What do you want to eat?"

She turned away.

"I'm ordering sushi," I said.

"I'm not hungry."

"I'll put yours in the fridge if you won't eat it."

After I ordered the food, I walked away into the living room and sat down on the couch and turned on the TV. Most of the effects of the alcohol had worn off, but I still felt slightly dizzy, especially sitting down.

A few minutes later Paula came into the living room and said, "It would make this much easier if you just admitted you have a problem."

"You're the one with the problem."

"You keep everything to yourself. You think if you keep it a secret it doesn't matter."

"Look who's talking about secrets. Who were you really having lunch with today?"

I was just trying to make a comeback, win a stupid point in an argument, but when I saw a flash of fear cross Paula's face I knew I'd hit on something.

"Why are you trying to change the subject?" she said.

"It was just a question. Why can't you answer it?"

Now Paula was looking down guiltily.

"I didn't want to tell you because I knew you'd make a big deal about it," she said. "And now you're *going* to make a big deal about it even though there's nothing to make a big deal about."

"What are you talking about?"

She looked at me, absorbing my gaze for a few moments, then said confidently, "I had lunch with Doug today."

"So you lied to me," I said.

"I didn't lie."

"You said you were having lunch with fucking Debbie."

"See? I knew you were going to blow this way out of proportion. It was nothing – nothing at all. Doug called me up at work today and wanted to meet. It turns out his firm has been recommending a company that I've done some research on – he wanted to get together to talk about it. I'm sorry I lied to you on the phone, but I knew you'd get upset and I didn't know what else to say. But that really was stupid of me and I'm sorry."

"So this was a *business* lunch?" I said.

"Yeah. I guess it was."

"You guess?"

"Come on, Richard, don't –"

"Did you fuck him?"

"*What?*"

"It was a simple question." I said slowly, "Did… you… fuck… him?"

"You're sick."

She started to walk away. I stood in front of her, blocking her.

"Get out of my way."

Trying to restrain myself, I took a long, deep breath and closed my eyes for a moment.

"I want to trust you right now," I said. "I really want to trust you."

"I don't know how we started talking about this anyway," she said. "This has nothing to do with me. This has to do with you and your drinking. You're just trying to turn it into something else."

"You still didn't answer my question."

"What question?"

"Did you fuck him?"

"I can't believe this."

"Did you fuck him?"

"Stop it!"

"Did you fuck him?"

"Shut up!"

I grabbed her by the shoulders and shook her.

"Did you fuck him? Did you fuck him? Did you fuck him?!"

"No!"

She tried to get away, to leave the living room, but I grabbed her again. She was struggling, pushing with her hands to get free. She turned toward the hallway. I didn't realize how close she was to the corner of the wall between the hallway and the living room. I also didn't realize how hard I pushed her. She stumbled backward, turning to brace herself, and the side of her head banged hard against the corner. For a moment or two she stood still, stunned, then she broke free and ran down the hallway into the bedroom, slamming the door behind her.

7

I pleaded at the bedroom door for Paula to let me in. I went on and on, telling her how sorry I was and how awful I felt, but she wouldn't answer me.

Finally, I gave up and went back into the living room and sat on the couch with my head in my hands. I couldn't believe that I'd pushed her so hard.

I put some ice in a towel and returned to the bedroom door. Paula still wouldn't let me in so I told her I was leaving the ice outside in the hallway and I walked away. Moments later, the door opened and Paula snatched the ice, then the door slammed closed and I heard the lock turn.

The sushi arrived. I didn't have an appetite so I put it away in the fridge.

I went back to the bedroom door and tried to convince Paula to let me inside.

"I just want you to know I love you very very much and I swear to God I'll never do anything like this again. You're right – I have a problem and I'm going to get help. Please – don't hold this against me. I'll never hurt you again – I promise. You have to believe me. Come on, please open up so you can see how sorry I am."

She didn't answer. I begged for a while longer, trying every possible approach, but nothing worked. Finally, I gave up and returned to the living room couch.

At six-thirty the next morning the bedroom door was still locked. I knocked quietly a few times, but there was no response. Then I said, "If you're awake, please let me in. You have to give me a chance to say I'm sorry."

She didn't answer. I walked Otis and made coffee. After pacing the apartment several times I returned to the door.

"Please," I said. "Come on, this is getting ridiculous. Please – just open the door."

Again, she didn't answer. It was past seven and I needed to get into the bedroom to get my clothes for work.

For the next ten minutes or so, I knocked on the door, trying to get her attention, gradually getting angrier. I knew she was just doing this to punish me, that she was going to keep me locked out of the bedroom until I was late for work.

At seven-thirty, I cursed and took a shower in the spare bathroom, washing my hair with soap. I had to leave for work by seven-forty at the latest because I had a nine o'clock appointment scheduled and I needed to stop by the office first to pick up some materials for my presentation. I banged on the door, demanding Paula to let me in.

"This is bullshit," I said. "I was wrong last night, okay, but you don't have to be a child about it. I said I was sorry, I admitted I have a problem, and now we have to go on with our lives. So just open the fucking door!"

I was so frustrated I half-considered breaking the door down, but I realized that would only make me seem crazier and more violent, and then it would be even harder to convince Paula to forgive me. Instead, I found an old, wrinkled suit in a bag of clothes Paula was planning to donate to a thrift shop and I ironed it quickly. It was still wrinkled, but it would have to do. I found a wrinkled shirt in the bottom of the closet, but I didn't have time to iron it. It didn't matter – I'd just keep the suit buttoned over it. As I was leaving the apartment I heard the shower running in the other bathroom. Obviously, Paula was planning to go to work today, but she wasn't going to leave the bedroom until *after* I was gone.

I took a cab across town. In my office, at my cubicle, I gathered the materials I needed for my meeting. Then I walked to Park and Forty-seventh to meet with the CFO of a small capital-management firm. As I gave my presentation, I was barely aware of what I was saying. I was too absorbed, thinking about Paula. I hoped she was okay and that she would eventually forgive me.

The meeting ended with the understanding that I would fax over a quote on the small networking project by the end of the week. I looked so disheveled and I was acting so distracted that I didn't see how I could have made a favorable impression.

Riding down in the elevator, I called Paula at her office on my cellphone. Her assistant answered, but when she heard my voice she apologized and said that Paula was "in a meeting" and couldn't come to the phone.

"Just transfer me to her," I said. "I was in an accident."

I thought I was convincing, but Paula was too smart and must have sensed the trick because her assistant returned and said, "I'm sorry, she won't... I mean she *can't* come to the phone right now. Would you like to leave a message?"

"I'll try back later," I said.

I went through the lobby of the building, out to the street. I was so absorbed in my thoughts that I was barely aware of the traffic and crowds. I went directly to Madison and Fifty-fourth and stood outside Michael Rudnick's building.

I didn't care if I had to wait all day – I had to see Rudnick again and this time I was going to confront him. I had no idea what I'd say, but I knew I had to say *something*.

It wasn't ten o'clock yet and I knew I'd probably have to wait until noon or later to see him. I sat on the ledge in front of the building. After a while, I took off my jacket and loosened my tie. I kept a close watch on the revolving doors, ready to get up as soon as I saw him. Then I had an idea. I remembered the name of the firm where he worked – Rudnick, Eisman and Stevens – and I took out my cellphone. I got the phone number from information and dialed. A receptionist answered and I asked if Michael Rudnick was in the office today. Rather than answering me, she transferred my call and a deep voice said, "Michael Rudnick."

I'd expected his secretary to answer, so hearing Rudnick's voice startled me. I held the phone up to my ear for a few more seconds, listening to him say "Michael Rudnick" in a louder, aggravated tone, then I hung up. I sat there for several more seconds, with the phone up to my ear, and then I realized that I was actually shaking. I put the phone away, angry at myself for being such a wimp.

I sat on the ledge for the next two hours. At noon, the lunch crowd started filing out of the building. If, for some reason, he decided not to go out for lunch today, I was planning to return to the building at four-thirty to catch him on his way home. If I missed him later, then I'd come back tomorrow and the next day, but eventually I was going to meet him face to face.

Then I saw him leaving the building. He was walking between a man and a woman, smiling, heading right in my direction. Suddenly, I felt the same immobilizing fear as when I'd heard his voice on the phone. As he approached, he put on the dark sunglasses that he was wearing the day I saw him crossing Fifth Avenue. He passed by without noticing me.

For a few moments, I couldn't move, then I forced myself to snap out of it, to get a grip. I stood up and followed Rudnick and his friends down Madison Avenue, across Fifty-third Street.

The sidewalk was crowded. The group turned left on Fifty-first and I followed, keeping about ten yards between us. In the middle of the block, they went into a Japanese restaurant. I stopped outside the door and watched a maître d' lead them to a table. I stood outside for a while, then I decided to go in. The maître d' was leading me toward the sushi bar when I noticed that the table next to Rudnick's group was empty. I asked the maître d' if I could sit there instead.

I sat in the seat closest to Rudnick. We were only a couple of feet apart, the backs of our chairs nearly touching. I realized that this was probably the closest I had been to him since the last time we were in his basement.

The restaurant was noisy, but I overheard snippets of the conversation behind me. Several times, I heard Rudnick refer to "the closing," so I assumed he was a real estate lawyer. I ordered two tuna rolls, one yellowtail roll, and two pieces of salmon. I remembered how I'd put the sushi I'd ordered last night away in the fridge and I realized that I hadn't eaten since yesterday afternoon.

I listened to the conversation behind me – now they were talking about the New York real estate market and I occasionally heard the name Trump. At one point, Rudnick started laughing loudly and it sickened me to hear him enjoying himself. I wondered what his friends at the table would say if they knew the truth. One thing for sure – Rudnick sure as hell wouldn't be laughing.

My food arrived. I devoured the sushi, barely tasting it, as I continued to eavesdrop on the boring conversation behind me. They must have remained at the table for a half-hour after they finished eating, talking about different real estate projects. Finally, Rudnick's deep voice boomed to the waiter several tables away, "Check, please!"

When the waiter looked over I said, "Mine, too."

Rudnick gave the waiter a credit card and I paid in cash. The waiter returned with my change and Rudnick's receipt. When I heard stirring behind me, I stood up as well. For a moment, Rudnick turned in my direction and his gaze swept past me.

Leaving the restaurant, I was trailing Rudnick so closely that I could smell his cologne. It was a different cologne than the one he wore as a teenager, but the odor was just as imposing.

I imagined reaching out and tapping him on the back and saying, "Remember me, asshole?"

I followed Rudnick and his friends back uptown on Madison Avenue, figuring they would go back into the building together. This meant I'd have to wait for another time to approach Rudnick – maybe later today or tomorrow. Then the group stopped at the corner of Fifty-fourth Street and they shook hands. I stopped and pretended to window-shop at some store, watching Rudnick's reflection in the glass. He walked away, alone, toward the entrance to his office building.

Suddenly, I had my chance to say something to him. As he continued up the block, I blurted out, "Hey, Michael Rudnick!"

Rudnick stopped and turned around, looking right at me. He wasn't wearing his sunglasses and he had a slightly confused expression. I probably looked vaguely familiar, but he hadn't put the whole picture together yet. Maybe he thought I was an old client or someone he knew from law school or college.

"You don't remember me, do you?" I said.

"Sorry," he said, squinting at me. "What's your name?"

"Richard," I said. "Or you probably remember me as Richie – Richie Segal."

At first, Rudnick's expression didn't change. Then I saw a flash of recognition cross his face. It was so fast if I wasn't looking for it I probably would have missed it, but in that moment I knew he remembered everything. It was great seeing the terror in his eyes as he wondered what I wanted from him. Then his mock-confused expression returned.

"I'm sorry," he said. "Where did we meet?"

I couldn't believe the arrogance of this asshole.

"I can't believe you don't remember me," I said. "You grew up in the house across the street from me."

He continued to stare at me, dumbfounded. He was chasing me around the Ping-Pong table, chanting, "You're gonna feel it! You're gonna feel it!" then he said, like it suddenly clicked, "Right, Richie Segal. It's been a long time, hasn't it? How did you recognize me?"

"I never forget a face," I said.

We stared at each other for a few awkward seconds then I looked down, noticing that he was wearing a thick gold wedding band. Rudnick said, "Well, *you've* definitely changed a lot. The last time I saw you you were what, ten years old?"

"You moved when I was twelve," I said.

"Oh – okay." He was looking away, distracted. I could tell he was uncomfortable and wanted the conversation to end. He looked at his watch and said, "Well, it was really terrific running into you again, but I'm running late for a meeting and I have to go. See you around."

He walked away and went into the building without looking back.

8

"Where have you been? I was looking all over for you."

I had just entered the bathroom, where Bob Goldstein was washing his hands.

"I had a sales meeting," I said.

"I looked at your calendar. Your meeting was at nine this morning, wasn't it?"

"It ran late and then we went to lunch. It went good, though."

"Did you close him?"

"Not yet, but I will."

"And what happened with your client from yesterday – the one with the one-day project?"

"He was upset we couldn't do it, but I'm not sure it's dead completely. I'll have to give him another call this afternoon."

"How about your other prospects? Anything hot in the cooker?"

"I have a few solid leads."

"Great. Let's hope this is your break-out week."

Bob wiped his hands with a paper towel and left the bathroom. I went to use the urinal. While I was washing up at the sink, Steve Ferguson came out of one of the stalls. He had been in there the entire time, eavesdropping on my conversation with Bob. He left the bathroom without looking at me.

I went back to my cubicle and logged on to my computer. Compared to dealing with Michael Rudnick, my problems at work suddenly seemed petty and inconsequential. I didn't really care anymore whether I closed a sale or if I was fired immediately. I'd had many jobs in the past and I'd have many jobs in the future. It really wasn't a big deal.

I called Paula at work – again her assistant answered

and again she refused to put my call through – then I started to search the internet to see if I could find any more information about Michael Rudnick.

I found six Michael Rudnicks. One had written a book on cystic fibrosis, one was a member of the swim team at the University of California, Davis, one was looking for interactive backgammon partners, one had won a handball tournament in Miami, one was an unemployed math teacher, and one co-owned a used-car dealership in Dayton.

Then I did a search for Rudnick, Eisman and Stevens and I found a reference to Michael J. Rudnick, Esquire. Unfortunately, the page dealt with the sale of office space in lower Manhattan, and didn't tell me anything I didn't already know.

I remembered how Rudnick had been wearing a wedding band. I wanted to know who his wife was, what she did for a living. I wanted to know if he had children and, if so, how old they were. I wanted to know where he lived. I remembered seeing the address the other day for a Michael Rudnick on Washington Street in the West Village. Washington Street was very far west, near the West Side Highway, in the meat-packing district, a primarily "gay neighborhood". Maybe Rudnick was gay and the wedding band meant that he had a husband.

My computer made a beeping sound, the signal that I had an email. It was from Bob, requesting a detailed list of all my outstanding proposals.

I deleted the message then went back to searching the net for information on Michael J. Rudnick.

I arrived home from work at a little after seven o'clock. The lights in the foyer and living room were on, but the bedroom door was locked again. I knocked softly. There was no answer, so I knocked again, a little harder.

"Come on, just open up," I said. "I don't want to have

to go through this nonsense again tonight."

I knocked again, then I heard footsteps and the door unlocking. I entered the room and saw Paula standing with her back to me, facing her closet. She was still in her work clothes – a conservative navy suit. I went up to her, stopping a few feet away.

"Look, I know there's absolutely nothing I can say to you right now," I said. "But you just have to know how sorry I am. I swear to God I'll never do anything like this again, and I –"

She turned around toward me. I was so startled I couldn't speak and I felt like crying. The left side of her face on and above her cheekbone was red and swollen, and the area under the eye was dark purple. I couldn't believe she'd gone to work looking that way.

"My God," I said. "I'm *so* sorry."

I tried to reach out to touch her, but she backed away.

"Stay the fuck away from me," she said.

"Look," I said. "I –"

"I'm telling you this once so you better not forget it," she said coldly. "If you ever, *ever* hurt me again the marriage is over. I don't care what you say or what excuses you make up. I'm not going to be one of those stand-by-their-man women who stay with their abusive, alcoholic husbands. Fuck that."

"I didn't mean to hurt you," I said.

"Don't give me that bullshit! You were trying to push me and you know it!"

I couldn't argue with this because it was the truth. I sat down on the bed and started to cry into my open hands. It was like I was at a funeral – my lips were quivering and I was short of breath. I knew this wasn't just about Paula. I was releasing stress and anger that had been building in me for days.

"You're going to A.A. and we're going to counseling," Paula said. "I called my therapist today and he recommended a Dr Lewis, a marriage counselor on Park Avenue. I made an appointment for Friday at six."

I continued to cry. I probably hadn't cried so much since I was a kid – Paula certainly had never seen me cry this way and it seemed to be having an effect on her. If I wasn't showing so much distress, she probably would have continued to yell at me. Instead, she stood in front of the bed for a while, then she sat down next to me, resting a hand on my knee. I knew she would have been acting very differently if she knew my crying had very little to do with her.

Finally, I stopped sobbing. Paula said, "I want to forgive you – I really do. I mean, I hurt you once and I know how important it was for me when you gave me a second chance. I want to do the same thing for you, but I want to tell you right now it's going to be very hard. What you did last night was so awful – it was the worst thing you could've done. What the hell's wrong with you?"

"I've been having a problem," I said.

"A problem? What kind of problem?"

I almost told her about Michael Rudnick. My lips started to move and a faint sound came out of my mouth, but I caugh myself just in time.

"There's just been a lot going on with me lately," I said.

"What do you mean?" she said. "You mean with your job? You've had problems at work before, but you've never acted like this."

"It's different now."

"Why?"

"It just is. I don't know why. Maybe it's a midlife crisis –"

"At thirty-four?"

"– or maybe it's just stress. Look, I know there's no excuse for what I did, all right? Maybe you're right – maybe I do have a drinking problem. I'll go to A.A. – I'll go into counseling with you if that's what you want. I'll do anything to get things back to normal with us."

I tried to hold her hand but she wriggled it free.

"Is there anything I can do for you?" I said. "Can I get you some more ice or something?"

"I'll be fine," she said. "It looked a lot worse this morning."

"What did people at work say?"

"I made up a story. I said I slipped coming out of the shower and fell against a towel rack. I think they believed me."

"You sure I can't get you something? Even something to eat?"

"I'll be okay – really. I'd just like to be alone for a while."

I changed out of my work clothes then went into the kitchen. I didn't have much of an appetite, but I decided I was probably starving and just didn't realize it. I took out the leftover sushi from the fridge and picked at it in the living room while I watched TV.

About a half-hour went by, then Paula came out of the bedroom. She took her sushi out of the fridge and sat on the chair adjacent to me and we watched TV together. We barely spoke. Several times, I tried to initiate conversation, but each time she had a curt, one-word response, and I realized that it was probably best to leave her alone – not push her. She would start talking to me again when she was ready.

Paula said she'd rather sleep alone, but at least this time she didn't lock me out of the bedroom. She let me take a spare blanket and pillow out of the closet to sleep with on the couch.

At around eleven o'clock, I walked Otis. When I returned to the building, I got into an elevator with a young boy. He was about thirteen years old and he had curly red hair. I had seen him many times over the past few years, in and around the building. Usually, he was with his mother or father, but now he was alone, holding a basketball. I remembered how I had been bouncing a basketball on the sidewalk, in front of my old house in Brooklyn, the first time Michael Rudnick invited me to his basement.

The boy's name was Jonathan. I didn't know why I knew this. I must have overheard his mother talking to him once.

"Have a good game?" I asked.

I had never spoken to the boy before and he double-taked before he said, "Yeah."

"Where did you play?"

"A schoolyard," he said shyly, and he looked up toward the illuminated floor numbers above the doors.

Staring at the boy, I imagined inviting him over to my apartment one day when Paula wasn't home to watch a basketball game on TV. We would make a bet – he would choose one team, and I would take the other. If his team won, I would give him five dollars. If my team won, I would give him a wedgie. Then, if I won the bet, I would chase him around the apartment, pull up his underwear, and pin him down on the couch.

I snapped out of it, suddenly aware of how the back of my neck was sweating.

The elevator doors opened on Jonathan's floor and he left without saying goodbye. I hoped he wouldn't tell his parents that some pervert had been leering at him in the elevator.

Later, standing in front of the bathroom mirror, I couldn't believe what was happening to me. First I'd pushed my wife into a wall *on purpose*, and now I was starting to have sick thoughts about preying on innocent boys.

I needed a glass of Scotch. I knew it was probably the wrong thing to do, but I couldn't stop myself. It was the only way I'd be able to relax, get back to normal. Besides, I'd only have one drink. What harm could one little drink do?

I made sure the door to the bedroom was still shut and then I opened the liquor cabinet quietly, only to discover that all the bottles were gone. I should have known that

Paula would do this. For a moment, I considered going outside again, to the deli on First Avenue, and buying a couple of beers, but I stopped myself, realizing that this was probably for the best. I had to get on the wagon sooner or later so I might as well start now.

Lying on the couch, I was sweating again. Unable to sleep, I turned on the TV with the volume muted. Otis climbed onto the couch and settled down next to my face. I petted him gently on his back and head and underneath his neck. It had taken me a while to get close with Otis. Originally, I'd wanted a cat, but Paula had her heart set on a cocker spaniel and, eventually, I gave in. I never thought I'd turn into one of those people who talked to their dogs on the street, but lately I had caught myself doing it all the time. And, right now, because I needed to tell somebody how I was feeling and there was nobody else to tell, I whispered into Otis's floppy ear: "I'm gonna kill him, Otis. I'm gonna kill that fucking bastard."

9

In the morning, I left a message on Bob's voicemail that I was sick and wouldn't be coming into work today. This was partly the truth because I'd been uncomfortable all night and I'd awakened with a sore throat, a stuffy nose, and a stiff neck. But even if I'd felt 100 percent I would have taken the day off.

Paula wasn't any more talkative then she had been last night. I was glad to see that her bruise had faded; underneath her make-up it would be barely noticeable.

I showered first and when Paula finished her shower I was already dressed in one of my work suits and was putting on my shoes. It was only seven-fifteen, but I told Paula I wanted to get a "head start" this morning. When I went to kiss her goodbye, she stepped back, not even letting me kiss her cheek.

It was raining hard, so I took an umbrella with me and left the apartment. I was in a hurry, so I took a cab across town to Madison and Fifty-fourth.

I was hoping to catch Rudnick on his way to work, figuring that, as a lawyer for a Madison Avenue firm, he must get to work very early. When the cab dropped me off I checked my watch and saw it was seven-thirty on the dot. I went to the spot near the main entrance where I had waited yesterday, except today the ledge was covered with puddles and I couldn't sit down.

For over an hour, I watched the streams of people entering the building. Almost everyone was carrying an umbrella, some at an angle against the wind, making it harder to see their faces.

As nine o'clock approached, the volume of people arriving for work increased, but there was still no sign of Rudnick. I wondered if he had come in already – some executives arrived at work before seven-thirty – and I was kicking myself for not leaving my apartment earlier.

At a few minutes after nine, I decided to call Rudnick's office on my cellphone. I said I was "Mr Jacobson, an old client of Michael Rudnick's," and Rudnick, the son of a bitch, took the call. I hung up immediately. Without another thought, I entered the building through the revolving doors and looked up Rudnick, Eisman and Stevens on the building's directory. When I got off the elevator on the thirty-second floor and approached the receptionist, I felt blood pulsing in my head.

"Michael Rudnick, please."

The receptionist stared at me as if I were frightening her.

"Do you have an appointment with him?" she finally asked.

"Just tell him an old friend is here to see him."

"I'm sorry," she said, still seeming slightly afraid. "I can't ask one of the lawyers to come to the desk without giving them a name."

I decided that the woman, who looked like she was about twenty-five, was probably a temp. A full-time employee wouldn't have referred to Rudnick as "one of the lawyers" and I knew that, if I kept being demanding, I could get her to do anything I wanted.

"Look, I'm a very close old friend of Michael's and I wanted to surprise him."

"Can't you just tell me your name?"

"It wouldn't be a surprise if he knew I was here."

The girl thought this over for a while then said, "Okay, he isn't with a client right now, so you can go inside… I guess."

The girl told me where Rudnick's office was – "straight back, all the way to the left" – and I thanked her for "helping me with the surprise".

I entered Rudnick's corner office without knocking, stopping a few feet in front of his desk. He was sitting there, reading some papers, and he looked up at me, completely startled.

Finally, he said, "What are you doing here?"

I didn't rush to answer. I stared at him for five, maybe ten seconds, wanting to milk this.

"What do you think I'm doing here?" I asked, smiling menacingly.

"The receptionist didn't tell me you were here," Rudnick said, as if this were his only problem with me suddenly appearing in his office. We continued to stare at each other until he said, "So what do you want?"

"Fuck you," I said.

I was losing control now, outside myself.

Rudnick stood up and came around the desk to face me. He was probably hoping he'd be able to intimidate me with his size, the way he used to. But now I was taller than him. He had forgotten this.

"Look, I don't know what the hell is wrong with you or what you think you're doing here, but if you don't get the hell out of here right now I'm calling security."

I shut the door so no one else could hear what was going on. When I turned back around, Rudnick was holding the telephone receiver up to his ear and had started dialing.

"Put the fucking phone down," I said.

He ignored me.

"I said put it down."

Now he was looking at me. "I told you to leave."

"I know what you did to me, you fucking son of a bitch," I said.

I heard a faint voice on the other end of the line, saying, "Hello," and then Rudnick hung up.

He continued to stare at me for what seemed like a very long time, but it might have only been a second or two, then he said calmly, "What the hell are you talking about?"

"Don't play dumb," I said. I wasn't *there* anymore. I was just a body with a voice coming out of it. I heard myself say, "You know exactly what I'm fucking talking about, you perverted fucking bastard."

Rudnick looked blank-faced, pretending to be completely confused. "Look, I don't know what you think you're doing here, or what's going on in your head –"

"'You're gonna feel it.' Do you remember saying that to me? Do you remember what you did to me afterwards?"

He was staring at me, still playing dumb.

"You're gonna feel it?" he said, as if he had no idea what I was talking about.

"How about chasing me around your Ping-Pong table?" I said. "How about pinning me down on the fucking couch?"

"Look, if you want to avoid a nasty scene, you can just turn around and leave here right now –"

"I'm not going anywhere until you admit what you did to me."

"What did I do to you?"

"You know exactly what you did."

"Look, I don't know what kind of problems you're having in your life right now," he said, as if he were speaking to an insane person, "but I'm not the answer. You obviously need help. So why don't you do yourself a favor and get the hell out of here?"

"Admit it," I said. "Admit it or I'm not going anywhere."

He reached back toward his desk, trying to get to the phone, but I stopped him, grabbing his shoulder from behind. He stuck out an arm to push me back, and the feel of his hand, pressing against my chest, set me off. I pushed him away and he stumbled backwards onto his desk. There was a loud noise – probably a paperweight falling onto the floor. I was yanking on the phone cord, but he wouldn't let go of the receiver. Then the cord suddenly freed and my momentum forced me backwards into someone who had just entered the room. Before I had time to think, huge dark-skinned arms were wrapped around my chest and a deep, angry voice was saying, "Calm down – just calm the fuck down, asshole."

The guy holding me back was a big black guy, apparently a maintenance worker in the building. Rudnick, with sweat covering his reddened face, ordered the man to throw me out of the office. As the man led me out, I yelled back at Rudnick, "You child-molesting bastard! You son of a bitch!"

The maintenance worker stood with me by the elevator, making sure I got on.

I walked downtown in the rain. Crossing Forty-second Street, I realized I had left my umbrella in Rudnick's office. It wasn't raining as hard as it had been this morning, but I had walked more than ten blocks and my suit was soaked. I continued walking downtown at a steady pace.

At Twenty-third Street, I veered onto Broadway, and I continued walking through the Village. It was raining hard again and my feet were sore, but I felt like I needed to keep moving. I was still worked up from the scene in Rudnick's office – I realized that I had probably gone into shock – and I was afraid that if I didn't work off my excess stress and anxiety I'd wind up craving a drink.

I had to pee, so I stopped in a church on Broadway and Tenth Street. After I went to the bathroom, I decided to rest and I sat down in one of the pews near the back. Organ music was playing at a low volume. There were several people scattered around the church, praying. An old woman sat alone to my left. A shawl was wrapped around her head and she was crying, rocking slowly back and forth. I stared at Jesus on the cross. Sometimes I thought that the idea of God existing was absurd, like believing in Santa Claus. Other times, I'd think about all the intelligent people in the world who believed in God – scientists, world leaders, scholars – and wonder how it was possible that all these people could be wrong.

When I was a kid, my mother used to drag me to church all the time. My father never liked the idea of my mother "forcing religion" on me, but my mother had more serious problems with my father. The real reason she went to church so often – besides Sundays, she went at least a few days during the week – was because she knew my father was cheating on her during his long business trips and she didn't know how else to handle it. I didn't figure out what was going on until I was about ten years old, when my friend Shawn told me that the little balloons we had been stealing from my father's suitcase were actually rubbers. Then I started eavesdropping on my father's hushed phone calls that he had only when my mother wasn't home, and I heard him telling some woman named Doris how sexy she was and how badly he wanted to be with her. After my parents finally divorced, my father never called me on my birthday and he tried to weasel out of paying child support.

Then I remembered all the times my father used to talk to Michael Rudnick on the street. My father liked Rudnick and often commented on what a "great, bright kid" he was. One time, I'd just come home from school and I saw my father and Rudnick, talking and laughing in Rudnick's driveway. It was during the period Rudnick was inviting me down to his basement to play Ping-Pong, but it never occurred to me to tell my father what was going on. Maybe I was just confused and didn't understand what was happening. Or maybe it was my fault – maybe if I'd told on Rudnick right away he would've been punished a long time ago. But how could I blame myself? I was just a kid. I was naive and afraid and I wanted to be liked. I already knew my father didn't like me, and Rudnick was so smooth and calculating that he used this against me. Rudnick knew I was vulnerable, that he could manipulate me however he wanted.

I stared at Jesus for another half-hour or so, then I got

up, passing the old woman who was still praying out loud, and went back out into the rain.

I had a big, painful blister on the bottom of my right foot. After soaking the foot in warm water in the bathtub for a while, I covered the blister with a Band-Aid and hobbled into the living room and settled in front of the TV.

It was about three-thirty in the afternoon. I'd walked all the way downtown, through Chinatown and the Wall Street area, to the Seaport, and back uptown on First Avenue. I was physically and mentally drained. I turned on the TV to some game show and fell right asleep.

I didn't wake up until Paula walked into the living room and Otis started barking.

"Hello," Paula said.

Still involved in a dream in which Paula and I were laughing, sitting next to each other on lounge chairs in the backyard of the house where I grew up in Brooklyn, her cold, angry tone confused me. Then I remembered the events of the past two days and I wished I were back in my happy dream.

"Hi," I said weakly.

Paula disappeared into the bedroom and I lay back down and started to doze. I had started to dream again when Paula returned to the living room, wearing shorts and a big white sweatshirt. I was glad to see that the bruise on her cheek was almost gone.

"Did you call A.A. today?"

It's hard to think fast when you're half-asleep, but luckily I had the wherewithal to say, "Yes."

"When are their meetings held?"

"There's one Monday."

"Isn't there one sooner?"

"No."

Apparently satisfied, Paula went into the kitchen. Thanks to my rapid heartbeat, I was wide awake. I felt bad for lying, but I knew Paula would be upset if I'd told her that I had completely forgotten about A.A.

Paula returned from the kitchen and asked me what I was in the mood for tonight – Chinese or Vietnamese.

"Vietnamese," I said.

She handed me the Vietnamese menu. I said I'd have the Saigon chicken, and she called the restaurant, ordering a grilled beef salad for herself.

When she got off the phone, Paula said, "I found out some good news today – my sister had a baby."

"Boy or girl?"

"Boy."

"Great."

There was a long, awkward silence. I was thinking how great it would be to have kids, yet how far Paula and I were from even discussing the idea.

Paula went back to the bedroom, then returned when the food arrived. We ate together at the dining table. Paula was slightly more talkative than last night, but things were still far from normal between us.

After dinner, we sat in the living room and watched the end of a bad made-for-TV movie. Paula reminded me that our counseling appointment was at six tomorrow evening, then she said goodnight, in a way that indicated there was no way in hell she was ready to sleep in the same bed with me.

Later on, alone on the couch, I tried to do what I had sworn I was going to do while I was walking home this afternoon – forget Michael Rudnick existed.

I turned off the TV and shut my eyes. I was back in Rudnick's basement in Brooklyn, underneath him on the black vinyl sofa. He was so heavy, I couldn't breathe. My face was pressed against the couch and I was crying. Then it was later that day. I was in the bathroom, staring at a wad of bloodstained toilet paper.

The memory ended and I still couldn't catch my breath.

I opened the door to the terrace, but exhaust from Third Avenue made me even queasier. I kneeled on the floor and put my head between my legs, finally starting to recover.

I had forgotten all about the toilet paper. I remembered telling my mother that my butt was bleeding and she had told me, "Don't worry about it, Richie. You probably just wiped too hard."

I feared that, if I returned to the couch, I would have another terrifying flashback, so I sat in the reclining chair and covered myself with the blanket. I couldn't sleep all night. Toward morning, dazed but wide awake, I came up with a plan.

By seven A.M. I'd already showered and was dressed for work, sitting at the snack bar in the kitchen, finishing a bowl of raisin bran. After breakfast, I went into the bathroom and poked my head into the shower stall where Paula was bathing and told her that I wanted to get a head start at work today and that I'd see her later on, at the marriage counselor's office. On my way out, I bent over and kissed Otis on top of his head, said, "See ya later, buddy," and headed out the door.

It was a clear, cool morning. I had plenty of time to get to work so I walked at a comfortable pace, arriving shortly before eight o'clock. I was heading down the corridor toward my cubicle when, from behind me, Bob said, "Richard, can I see you in my office for a sec?"

"Sure," I said.

I made a U-turn and followed Bob into his office. He'd sounded particularly serious and unfriendly and I wondered what could be wrong. I didn't think my job was in jeopardy, given that I was finally starting to generate some serious leads.

Bob sat at his desk. He stared at me for a few seconds, like a disappointed parent, then he said, "Where were you yesterday?"

"What do you mean?" I said. "I left a message on your voicemail – didn't you get it? I took a sick day."

"So you were home all day?"

I nodded. Bob smiled, shaking his head. I felt like I was the butt of an inside joke.

"Heidi saw you yesterday morning on Madison Avenue. She said you were in a suit and tie. What were you doing, going out on job interviews?"

"What difference does it make where I was?" I said.

"Look, I believe in honesty, all right?" Bob said. "No bullshit, no beating around the bush. Do you want to work for this company or don't you?"

"Yes," I said.

"Then act like it," Bob said. "You're not exactly producing as it is, then you start calling in sick, going on job interviews –"

"I wasn't going on job interviews."

"Then what were you doing?"

"If you really want to know, I was at a doctor's appointment."

"I don't believe you."

"It's true."

"What was wrong with you?"

"I'll tell you, but it's kind of embarrassing... I have hemorrhoids."

"Hemorrhoids?"

"Yes, and actually it's a very bad case. Just sitting here now is killing me."

"Look, Richard," Bob said seriously. "I think I've been very fair with you since you've been here, don't you? The least you could do is be fair with me in return."

"I don't understand what I did wrong."

"I don't want to get into a big blaming match, all right? I really don't care if you have hemorrhoids or if you don't have hemorrhoids. The bottom line is I need salesmen at this company who want to be here, who won't let personal issues affect their performance. I know you were upset that we couldn't service your prospect the other day and that you lost your office, but that's just the way the ball bounces. You have to go with the flow, be a mensch. You make a very nice base salary here – start showing me you deserve it. I can't have any negativity on the sales force. Negativity is a disease – one guy has it and before you know it the whole company is infected. I want to kill the disease before it spreads. This is your final warning, Richard. I don't know what's going on in your head, but I really hope you start taking this job seriously."

There was a lot I could have said, but I was smart enough to keep my mouth shut.

I returned to my cubicle and stayed there for the rest of the morning. At twelve o'clock sharp, I left for lunch, although eating was probably the last thing on my mind. Carrying my briefcase, I took the D train downtown to Macy's on Thirty-fourth Street. I went upstairs to the ninth floor and had a salesman fit me with a ready-to-wear wig. It had straight, dirty blond locks that went over my ears. Looking in a mirror, I barely recognized myself, but the additional hair didn't look silly on me either. My hairline had been receding lately anyway, and the wig was actually a major improvement in my appearance. It made me look at least five years younger, but more important, it made me look different. The salesman suggested that I might want to try another color, but I told him it was just what I was looking for and I paid for it in cash.

To complete the disguise, I went downstairs to the ground floor and bought a pair of dark, mirrored sunglasses.

I put the sunglasses along with the wig inside my briefcase and went outside. From a payphone on Thirty-fourth Street, I called Rudnick's office. I asked if Michael Rudnick was in today, claiming that my name was Joseph Ryan, an old client of his. The receptionist said that yes, he was in today, and I hung up. I headed back toward my office. When I got off the subway at Forty-seventh Street, I stopped at a deli and bought a BLT. I still didn't have an appetite, but I didn't want to get hungry later in the afternoon.

I ate part of the sandwich in my cubicle, then I tried to get back to work. But it was even harder to concentrate now than it had been earlier in the day. In the morning, I'd added a bogus "4:00 meeting" to my schedule so that I'd be able to leave the office early, without any hassle. At 3:45, I clocked out with my swipe card and headed down to the street. I entered the lobby of the GE Building and went directly to a public men's room. Inside a stall, I put on the wig and the sunglasses. I checked myself out in the mirror above the sink, delighted to see that my disguise looked just as natural and convincing as it had at Macy's. I exited the building at Rockefeller Center and headed across town toward Madison Avenue.

It was a little after four o'clock and I was standing outside Michael Rudnick's building, watching the revolving doors. As five o'clock approached, more people began to exit the building. I didn't see Rudnick, but I knew that attorneys very often stayed late at work, and some didn't leave their offices until eight or nine at night, or later.

By 5:45, the exodus from the building was diminishing, and I realized that I could be in for the long haul. I also realized that now there was little or no chance that I'd be able to make it to the marriage counselor's office in time for the six o'clock appointment. I called information on my cellphone and got Dr Michelle Lewis's phone number, then I left a message on her voicemail, saying that I couldn't make the appointment and to please tell my wife how sorry I was. I knew that Paula was going to give me hell later, but I would just have to deal with it.

At a few minutes past six o'clock, I called Rudnick's office from a payphone at the corner, looking back over my shoulder to make sure I didn't miss him. His voicemail answered. I hoped this didn't mean he had gone home for the day. Maybe he was just in a meeting or away from his desk.

It was nearing dusk. The crowds on the street had thinned and many of the stores on the avenue had closed. I was about to go back to the payphone, to call his office again, when I saw him.

He had just exited the revolving door and was heading toward the street at a brisk pace. I knew my disguise worked, because he passed by me without even looking in my direction. His smug, self-absorbed attitude and the way he was strutting along the street, like he thought he was a movie star, disgusted me.

I followed him downtown on Madison and then we made a right on Forty-eighth Street. We were heading toward the intersection on Fifth where I had spotted him last week. I was about twenty or so yards behind him, walking at his same, rapid pace. There were several people between us, but he was in full view. No matter what, I wasn't going to let him out of my sight.

We crossed Fifth and Sixth and were heading toward Seventh. On Seventh he made a left, continuing downtown. He was probably heading toward Washington Street in the West Village, where one of the Michael Rudnicks I had found on the internet lived. It was twilight, meaning that, by the time we reached Rudnick's apartment, it would be completely dark.

At Forty-second Street, I expected him to head down to the subway, but he continued downtown instead. It seemed as if he was planning to walk home, which would be kind of strange considering we still had about fifty blocks to go.

We passed Macy's on Thirty-fourth Street, where I had been earlier in the day. Then, at Thirty-third Street, Rudnick crossed the avenue and headed into Penn Station.

At first, I thought he was going to take the subway after all, but he passed the escalator that led to the subway and went toward the area where the New Jersey Transit and Amtrak trains departed. Without stopping, he glanced at the overhanging board that displayed the departure and arrival times, then he began to walk faster toward one of the escalators leading to one of the tracks. I followed him, jogging to keep up.

At the bottom of the escalator, he boarded a New Jersey Transit train and I entered at the other end of the car, making it inside just before the doors closed. I watched Rudnick sit down near the front of the car and I found a seat five or six rows behind him.

Taking a trip to New Jersey definitely hadn't been part of my plan, but there was no turning back now. I couldn't stop staring at the back of Rudnick's head.

As the train approached the Newark station, the conductor came by and asked me for my ticket. I told him that I needed to purchase one and I asked him what the last stop on the train was. "Trenton," he said, and I said, "One round-trip to Trenton."

When the train stopped, a number of people stood up and crowded the aisle. I watched Rudnick closely, but he remained seated, reading a newspaper.

The stations on the New York–Trenton route were about ten minutes apart. At each stop, many more passengers exited the train than entered, and when we reached Metuchen, about forty minutes from Manhattan, there was only about a dozen people left in the car, including Rudnick and myself.

It was much quieter on the train now, making my thoughts seem much louder.

At the Edison and New Brunswick stops, several more people exited. Now there were only a handful of passengers left in our car and I knew there couldn't be many more stops before Trenton. As the train slowed, approaching the Princeton Junction station, Rudnick stood up and headed toward the exit door nearest to him, at the end of the car. Not wanting to trail him too closely, I stood up and waited near the middle door. When the train stopped and the doors opened I made sure Rudnick had gotten off, and then I followed him toward the exit at the middle of the outdoor platform.

As he walked ahead of me, down the staircase, I started to feel disoriented, the way I sometimes felt after a few drinks. It was hard to see clearly in my sunglasses, but I left them on anyway. Rudnick went through a tunnel, passing under the tracks, and there was the noise above us of the train pulling out.

I was about to do it right there, in the tunnel, but then I heard echoing high-heeled footsteps. Looking over my shoulder, I saw a woman following about ten yards behind me.

Rudnick emerged from the tunnel and headed toward the dark parking lot. There were several cars with their motors running, waiting to pick up passengers from the train. For a moment, I feared that Rudnick would get into one of the cars, but then he veered left toward the darkest part of the lot.

The lot was half-filled with parked cars, but there didn't seem to be any people close by. I walked faster to keep up, trying not to make any noise. Rudnick turned to the right, between a row of cars. He must have heard me, because he stopped suddenly and turned around.

Except for some light from a nearby lamppost that cast a faint orange glow on Rudnick's face, the parking lot was dark. There was some noise of traffic in the distance. I saw Rudnick squinting, as if trying to figure out who I was. I was still walking toward him and then I stopped a few feet away.

"I'm sorry," he said, still straining to see. "Can I help you?"

Then his eyes widened and the puzzled expression disappeared.

Now he looked terrified.

"What the hell are *you* doing here?"

He was smiling with his caterpillar eyebrows and his faceful of acne, yelling, "You're gonna feel it! You're gonna feel it!"

I had taken the butcher knife out of my briefcase and I was lunging forward. Most of the blade entered Rudnick's chest and his terrified expression returned. I kept attacking, pushing him against a car and yanking the blade free, then sticking it in again. His shocked, wide-open eyes were looking right at me now. I stabbed him again, higher in his chest, closer to his neck.

He tried to speak, but blood choked his words. I worked the blade free, noticing that his eyes had shut. I let go, letting his limp body fall onto the concrete between two cars.

A train was speeding by, probably an Amtrak on the express track, and there was a sudden thunderous *whoosh*. I kneeled down and gave Rudnick one final stab, in the groin. After wiping the blade clean on his pants legs, I put the knife away in my briefcase and headed back toward the train station.

10

I keeled over between two parked cars and gagged. I remained in the same position for about a minute – the sick, sour taste of a partially digested BLT in my mouth – but I didn't throw up.

Finally, I felt better. I took off my bloodstained suit jacket and put it away in my briefcase, figuring I'd get rid of it later. There was still blood on my hands and on the bottoms of my shirtsleeves. I took off my shoes and socks. I spat on the socks, making them moist, then I wiped my face and neck, just in case there was blood there. I wiped my hands on the socks, removing as much blood as possible. Finally, I put the stained socks inside my briefcase. Then I folded each shirtsleeve several times, hiding the stains. In the poor light, it was hard to see if I had any blood on my pants; I was sure there was some there, but my pants were dark navy and I hoped the color camouflaged it.

I checked myself carefully. As far as I could tell, I looked fine. My hands, especially the palms, were still pink, but that would be easy enough to hide. I straightened my wig and adjusted my sunglasses, then I continued toward the light of the train station.

Much calmer now, feeling almost normal, I went up the stairs that led to the New York-bound track. As I was nearing the top, a man in a business suit headed down, passing to my right. I looked away as soon as I saw him, making sure he didn't get a good look at me.

I walked along the platform, past the ticket office and a bench where a few people were seated. I would have gone in the other direction, but I wanted to board the last car of the next train, where there were likely to be fewer passengers than on the other cars. As I passed the people,

I kept my head turned toward the tracks, enough so that my face was out of view.

The end of the platform was empty. I leaned over the edge and saw a train's headlights in the distance. It was hard to tell how far away the train was because this area of New Jersey was almost flat to the horizon. I paced back and forth, whispering, "Come on, come on, come on." Then I decided that I ought to stand still – if I looked nervous it could raise suspicion later. I couldn't hear traffic noise anymore and the silence was ominous. At any moment, I expected to hear screaming and commotion.

The platform was better lit than the parking lot and I noticed a big blotch of blood that I'd missed on my briefcase. I looked toward the ticket office to make sure no one was coming, then I crouched near the back of the platform. I took one of the socks out of the briefcase and wiped away as much blood as I could. Then there was a screeching of brakes – a train was arriving on the Trenton-bound track. I put the sock back into the briefcase and stood up, trying to act as natural and unassuming as possible. I could see the profiles of several people in the windows of the train, but no one was looking in my direction.

As the train left the station, I leaned over the tracks to see if the New York-bound train was any closer. The bright lights in the distance looked the same as before. I was going to have to brace myself now because I knew that some of the people who had just arrived at Princeton Junction would be going to their cars and there was a chance Rudnick would be discovered at any moment.

Then I had something else to worry about. I looked toward the opposite platform and saw a young woman standing there, searching for something in her pocketbook. This wouldn't have been a big deal except that she sensed me staring at her and looked in my direction. Reflexively, I smiled and she smiled back at me. I looked away immediately, cursing to myself for being so stupid, but when I looked again the woman was still there, smiling.

My heart skipped at least a beat. Casually, I walked about ten yards, toward the middle of the platform. I looked to my left, surprised to see that the woman had also walked about ten yards in the same direction. I stopped and watched the woman continue along the platform and exit down the stairs.

The noise of the train to New York, pulling into the station, was a big relief. I just wanted to get on the train and get away as fast as possible and worry about everything else later.

As the train slowed to a stop, I walked quickly back toward the end of the platform and boarded the last car. The train was more crowded than I had expected – filled with loud teenagers in ripped jeans and T-shirts, probably on their way to a concert or a club. I found a seat near the back of the car. It seemed like it took forever for the doors to close, but they finally did and the train started moving. I looked over my shoulder toward the parking lot, but the window had fogged and it was impossible to see out.

Although I was glad to get away from Princeton Junction, I knew my problems were far from over. It wouldn't be long before the body was discovered and if Rudnick had told anyone in his office what my name was, the police would track me down and make me their prime suspect.

The kids on the train were getting louder, but they were so involved in their own excitement that they didn't seem to notice me. I became aware of a faint odor of pot and one of the kids – tall, thin, probably about sixteen, with bad skin – was drinking from a bottle of beer, poorly concealed by a paper bag.

After the train left the New Brunswick station, the conductor entered the car. I'd wedged my ticket into the slot on top of the seat ahead of mine and I looked down when the conductor approached, trying not to make eye contact with him. After he collected my ticket and replaced it with a white card indicating how far I'd be traveling on the train, he said, "I think your face is bleeding, pal."

I don't know how I managed to stay calm. I imagined authorities from Princeton Junction calling the train and alerting them that a murder suspect might be on board. Afraid that I would appear even more suspicious if I kept looking down, I glanced up at the conductor for a moment, taking his image in quickly – tall, heavyset, with a mustache – and said, "Thanks, must've cut myself shaving."

I had no idea how much blood there was on my face and whether this excuse would sound ridiculous or not, but the conductor seemed satisfied because he went to collect the teenagers' tickets without another word. I moved close to the window, studying the reflection of my face, and was relieved to see that there was only a tiny streak of blood above my right cheekbone that I must've missed when I'd wiped my face with the sock. I licked my hand to wipe the blood clean and had to lick it again when it didn't come off the first time. Realizing that the salty taste in my mouth was Michael Rudnick's blood, I gagged, but fortunately I didn't throw up.

The scare was over, or at least I hoped it was. The blood was gone from my face and the conductor had left the car without glancing at me again. He had no reason to be suspicious, but I realized how easily that could change.

The one-hour-or-so trip back to the city seemed endless, but the train finally pulled into Penn Station. I knew I had to get home fast so I'd have as little missing time to account for as possible.

Rather than waiting upstairs on the "taxi line" where it was well lit, I decided to hail a cab on the street. I exited onto Eighth Avenue and a cab stopped for me right away. I told the driver my destination, "Sixty-second and Lex," purposely choosing a corner several blocks from my apartment, on the off-chance he might be questioned about it.

I was hoping not to have any more conversation with the driver but unfortunately he was a "talker." He went into a maniacal, rambling monologue about politics, baseball, sex, and movies. Even though I was ignoring him, he didn't get the message and kept blabbing away, nonstop, until he pulled over on the corner of Sixty-second and Lexington to let me out.

After exiting the cab, I ducked into a vestibule on East Sixty-second Street and took off my wig and sunglasses and put them away with the other evidence in my briefcase. It was ten-thirty as I walked at a brisk pace toward my apartment building. I was becoming more and more confident that everything would work out and that the police wouldn't catch me. It was a Friday night, which would work to my advantage. I had once read somewhere that almost all arrests take place during the first twenty-four hours of an investigation. Since the police probably wouldn't have a chance to talk to the people in Rudnick's office until Monday, the entire trail would have more than two full days to cool off. By Monday morning, the cab driver, the conductor, and the woman on the opposite platform, or anyone else who might have seen me tonight,would be less likely to remember me.

Entering my building, I smiled and said hello to Raymond, the evening doorman, like I would do on any normal night, and then I casually went to the mailbox area. There was no mail in my box, meaning that Paula was probably home. I was expecting her to be waiting for me at the door, with her hands on her hips, ready to lay into me for not showing up at the marriage counselor's office. I knew that a huge argument was inevitable, but I was hoping to put it off for as long aspossible, or at least until I had a chance to get rid of the murder evidence from my briefcase.

The lights were out in the apartment and Otis didn't come to the door to greet me. The bedroom door was closed, meaning Paula was probably locking me out for the night again. But I knew I had to play this right. I had to act like I wanted her to open up, otherwise it might raise suspicion later.

I knocked on the bedroom door for a few minutes, saying, "Come on, let me in," and telling her how "sorry" I was, and how I could "explain everything." Of course, she didn't respond, which was perfectly fine with me. I went to the kitchen with my briefcase and took out the butcher knife. I would've gotten rid of it, dumped it somewhere, but I knew Paula would miss it. I started to scrub the knife under hot water. Blood covered most of the blade and the handle and some of it had hardened, forming a dark, scablike substance. The sink filled with a shallow puddle of pink water and I was getting nauseous again. I didn't mind the blood, I minded that it was *Rudnick's* blood and that he wasn't completely out of my life yet. Until every last drop of him was gone I knew I would feel slightly sick.

Finally, all the visible blood was gone and the water in the sink had faded to a barely noticeable pink tinge. I kept scrubbing for a few minutes longer, just in case there were any microscopic droplets I'd missed, and then I dried the knife with a dishtowel and replaced it in the drawer.

Next, I took a plastic shopping bag from The Gap out of the cupboard below the sink and filled it with the bloody socks, the wig, the sunglasses, and the suit jacket. Then I unbuttoned my shirt and took off my pants and shoes and added them as well. Blood had stained some papers and folders in my briefcase, but I knew that it probably wasn't a good idea to dump anything personal with the clothes, so I left the papers alone, figuring I would get rid of them later.

"Where were you?"

Holding the plastic bag, I turned around and saw Paula

113

standing by the kitchen door, facing me. I had no idea how long she had been there. For all I knew she had seen me handling the bloody clothes and papers.

"When?" I asked, aware of my pulse throbbing in my face.

"I'm not in the mood for any more bullshit," she said. "Why weren't you at the marriage counselor's today? Did you just blow it off or do you have some other excuse?"

"I was at a bar... drinking," I said meekly.

"That's what I figured," she said.

I was about to go on, apologizing, but she cut me off with:

"I'm moving out."

I couldn't believe it.

"Come on," I said. "I know you don't –"

"Please," she said, "I'm not in the mood to discuss it. Tomorrow I'm moving to a hotel. Goodnight."

Paula marched down the hallway, then I heard the bedroom door shut and lock. Normally, I would have gone after her and tried to talk some sense into her, but now I was just glad to have her out of the way. Of course, I didn't want her to leave me, but I figured that this wasn't exactly the time to try and save my marriage.

Paula had let Otis out of the bedroom and now he came up to me and started sniffing the plastic bag.

"Easy, boy," I said, afraid he'd start to bark.

I took the bag with me into the bathroom, where I washed my face, hands, and arms thoroughly. Then I changed into sweatpants and a T-shirt that I'd pulled out from the top of the laundry.

I came out of the bathroom, put on a pair of sneakers, and leashed Otis. In the hallway, waiting for the elevator, Otis was still trying to sniff the bag.

Passing Raymond, I said, "Great weather, huh?" and he said, "Yeah."

This was part of my plan too – engage Raymond in small

talk, to distract him from noticing that I was holding the bag.

I was still counting on the police not questioning me, but if they did I wanted to make sure that I had taken care of every loose end.

Usually, I walked Otis down the block, to Second Avenue and back, but this time I crossed Second and walked farther east. Otis seemed to sense that something unusual was going on. Normally, he was playful and excited during his walks, sniffing every object we passed, running ahead of me, tugging on the leash. But tonight he walked calmly by my side, as if he knew that this was no time to joke around.

After First Avenue, East Sixty-fourth Street became darker and more deserted. My idea was to dump the bag in a garbage can somewhere. Even though this was very risky – a homeless person could find it, open it, and perhaps dump the contents onto the street – it seemed less dangerous than getting rid of it in the trash compactor in my building, where the evidence could easily be linked to me. Then I spotted a Dumpster at the curb in front of a building. It was half-filled with wood and other debris, but no one would pay any attention to one harmless plastic bag. I flung the bag over the side, watching it drop safely out of view.

I returned to my apartment and immediately went to work, cleaning out the rest of my briefcase. I took a big pot from the stove in the kitchen and, along with the bloody papers and folders from the briefcase and a book of matches, I went out to the terrace. I ripped the papers and folders into small pieces and ignited them in the pot. The blaze created a greater rush of gray smoke then I'd expected, but it was a breezy night and the cloud dispersed quickly. I waited for the ashes to cool down, then I took the pot into the bathroom and dumped the ashes into the toilet and flushed them.

Back in the kitchen, I wiped down the inside and outside of the briefcase. I was starting to get excited, knowing that I was almost done. I ran through a mental checklist three or four times, making sure I hadn't forgotten anything, then I went into the bathroom and took a shower. Looking up at the shower head, with the hot water spraying against my face, I finally felt free.

Later, I relaxed on the couch in the living room and closed my eyes. It was a relief to see pure darkness, not to be terrorized by the past.

I made a chirping noise with my tongue against the roof of my mouth, beckoning Otis, and then I said, "Here, puppy," but he didn't respond. He was probably still under the kitchen table, where he had been hiding since we'd come home from our walk.

11

"You have to give me another chance. I know I've been a big jerk lately, there's no question about that, but I can change – I *have* changed. I promise – from now on, things'll be different. I'll go to marriage counseling, I'll go to A.A. – I'll do anything I have to do to keep you from leaving me. Please. I'm begging you."

It was morning and I was in the foyer, standing between Paula and the door. She was wearing jeans and a suit jacket, holding a small suitcase.

"I'm sorry," she said. "I gave you another chance and you blew it." "Look," I said, blocking her as she tried to sidestep past me. "I know I have a problem, but I'm going to deal with it now – I swear I will. I know you don't have any reason to trust me, and if I were you I'd probably feel the same way, but give me a second chance and I promise I won't fuck up again. You screwed up one time and I forgave you, didn't I? The least you can do is do the same thing for me now."

Paula was staring at me without blinking. She was still upset, but my last words had definitely hit home.

Finally, she said, "How can I trust you? I mean we've been through all this before."

"I was an asshole, what can I say? But I'm begging you – I won't screw up again. Just give me one more chance. That's all I ask. Please, honey. Please."

Paula looked at me wide-eyed for at least ten seconds, then she said, "Fine, I won't move out today, but this is it – your last chance. Fuck up one more time, I'm out the door."

"Thank you," I said. "I love you so much. Thank you."

She went to the bedroom and returned without her suitcase.

"I'll see you later," she said.

I was in the living room, folding the sheet and blanket.

"Where are you going?" I asked.

"To my office," she said.

"On Saturday?"

"I need to prepare for a meeting next week."

"When will you be home?"

"I have no idea."

When she was gone, I went right into my office in the spare bedroom, turned on my PC, and logged on to the internet. First, I checked the *Times* online edition, but I couldn't find any mention of a murder in New Jersey. Technically, it would be an out-of-town news story, but it seemed likely that the New York papers would run a story about the murder of a lawyer from a prominent Madison Avenue firm.

I went to Netscape News and did a search for "murder," "Princeton," and "New Jersey." Two results appeared:

MAN STABBED AT PRINCETON TRAIN STATION

NEW JERSEY STAB VICTIM FIGHTS FOR LIFE

I caught my breath and opened the first news item. When I read how the stab victim, thirty-nine-year-old real estate attorney Michael Rudnick of Cranbury, New Jersey, was in critical-but-stable condition at St. Francis Medical Center in Trenton, my entire body went numb. It seemed impossible – there had to be some mistake. I had stabbed him so many times, and he had lost so much blood – there was no way he could have possibly survived. Yet, according to the article, that was exactly what had happened.

I skimmed the rest of the story, but I was such a mess I didn't understand what I was reading and I had to reread it. Finally, after several tries, the words started to make sense. Rudnick had been discovered late yesterday evening at around 10:15 P.M., about the same time I had arrived in Penn Station. Apparently, he was "near death" when paramedics arrived on the scene. Police offered no details about the case except that they were conducting "a thorough investigation."

The second article contained pretty much the same information as the first, except for a quote from a police spokesperson, stating that "detectives have several leads." There was no mention in either story about whether Rudnick had been conscious or not at the time he was taken to the hospital. I hoped that "near death" meant he was unconscious, because if he was awake the first words out of his mouth would have been my name. For all I knew he had already told the police about me, which would explain why they suddenly had "several leads."

I knew I was going to get caught – it was only a matter of time. I imagined the police coming to take me away, and the embarrassment and humiliation I would feel, being led out of the building in handcuffs.

I read the first article again, focusing on the mention of how Rudnick's body had been discovered yesterday evening at ten-fifteen. I decided that, since that was almost twelve hours ago, it was unlikely Rudnick had been conscious when he arrived at the hospital. If he *had* regained consciousness, the police probably would have tracked me down by now. This gave me some hope, but not much.

As I scrolled through the second article again I suddenly realized what an idiot I was – using the internet, with my *own* account, to search for information about the man I'd killed last night. Why didn't I just leave my fingerprints or a piece of paper with my name and address on it on Rudnick's body? Then I convinced myself that it probably didn't matter, that the police wouldn't go to the trouble of investigating my searches. First, they would have to somehow figure out that I'd used Netscape, and then they would have to request all kinds of information from my internet service provider. Still, I wished I'd gone to a Net cafe, or hadn't gone online at all.

After I erased all the history files and temporary internet files from my PC, I went into the living room and turned on the TV to New York 1, the twenty-four-hour-a-day cable news station.

After about ten minutes, a report about the stabbing came on. A recent picture of Rudnick was shown as the anchorman rehashed the information that I had read on the internet.

Desperate for more news, I turned on the stereo to an all-news radio station. At the top of the hour, the anchorman announced the headlines, which included "New York lawyer stabbed in New Jersey". I paced the living room, waiting for the full report. Finally, after several other stories, the anchorman gave some basic information about the stabbing and then a reporter came on the air, live from the Princeton Junction train station. The reporter, in a grim tone, said that Michael Rudnick had been discovered, bleeding profusely from multiple stab wounds, at about ten-fifteen last evening by Mark Stevens and Connie Cordoza, a young couple who were returning from Manhattan. Then the feed switched to Stevens's recorded comments: "I saw something and I said to my girlfriend, 'I think there's a dead guy there,' and she was like, 'No way.' So then I went up to it and I saw all the blood and we just, like, ran for help. We just ran."

I remained kneeling in front of the speakers, waiting for the next update, praying for Rudnick to die. Every half-hour or so the news stories about the stabbing in Princeton were repeated, and it was like a recurring nightmare, listening to the same reporter on the scene give the same details about the attack, and listening to the same account of the couple who had discovered Rudnick alive. I heard the report five times, meaning I had been in virtually the same position on the floor for over two hours.

Finally, I got up to go to the bathroom. Standing over the bowl, I heard a buzzer sound. I was convinced it was the police coming to arrest me, but then I realized that the buzzer of another apartment had sounded and the noise had come through the vent above the toilet.

When I returned to the living room, the reporter at Princeton Junction was saying, "… at this time the police are releasing no other details, other than that their investigation is ongoing and that they are exploring several leads. Once again, Michael Rudnick, the lawyer who was stabbed yesterday evening in the parking lot of the Princeton Junction New Jersey Transit station, has regained consciousness and police plan to question him shortly."

I knew that my only chance now was to make a run for it. Maybe I could hide out somewhere, change my identity, contact Paula when it was safe.

I started packing a suitcase in the bedroom – stuffing in some shirts, underwear, pants, socks, and whatever else my hands could grab – when I stopped, suddenly exhausted, realizing that running away was pointless. If the police knew who I was and had a description of me I'd never make it out of the city.

I returned to the living room and collapsed on the couch. I remained that way for hours, barely moving. Finally, I fell asleep. When I opened my eyes, the apartment was dark. I heard dishes clanging in the kitchen – Paula was home. Poor Paula. When the news broke that her husband had tried to kill a man in cold blood, her life would be ruined. If she thought she was screwed up now and needed therapy, wait until tomorrow.

I still didn't have the energy to move. I figured it must be eight or nine o'clock, but I didn't feel like lifting my arm to check my watch. I didn't know what was taking the police so long. Maybe Rudnick was still with his doctors, and the police had to wait to question him.

"Are you going to lie there on the couch all day?" Paula asked.

I hadn't even noticed her enter the room.

I didn't answer her.

"Whatever," she finally said. She walked away only to return a few seconds later. She said, "What's going on here anyway? Are you drunk?"

Again I didn't say anything.

"If you're drunk again," she said, "after everything you told me –"

"I'm not drunk," I said. My voice was deep and hoarse because I hadn't spoken in hours.

"Then what's wrong?"

"Nothing's wrong."

"Then why is there a suitcase on the bed?"

I waited several seconds, then I said, "I don't know."

"What do you mean, you don't know? There's a suitcase on the bed with clothes in it. Were you planning to go somewhere?"

I closed my eyes.

"Fine, you don't want to talk to me, don't talk to me. I'm sick of this shit."

She started to walk away, then I said, "Maybe I'm just depressed."

"Then take some Prozac or see a shrink," she said. "Stop acting like such a goddamn baby."

I remained on the couch, staring at the dark ceiling. Paula went into the bedroom and I heard the occasional faint canned laughter of the sitcom she was watching.

I turned on the TV with the remote and watched the New York 1 news. It was nine o'clock. A female reporter, live on the scene outside the hospital in Trenton, said that the police had spoken with Rudnick and had received an account of what had happened last night at the Princeton

Junction parking lot. I was expecting to hear my name, but the reporter said that a white teenaged boy with a ponytail and a goatee had attacked Rudnick in an attempted mugging, and that a statewide manhunt for the teenager was already under way.

12

I needed to get out of the apartment. I walked a few blocks to the East River, and then headed up the promenade alongside the FDR Drive. Besides a few joggers, drunks, homeless people, and an occasional couple taking an evening stroll, the promenade was empty. It was a cool night and a refreshing breeze was coming in off the river. After about twenty minutes of walking, I reached Gracie Mansion. I turned around and headed back, still replaying the events of the past twenty-four hours in a frantic blur.

Last night, the parking lot had been poorly lit, but there was enough light for Rudnick to see my face and by the way he'd asked "What the hell are *you* doing here?" there was no doubt he'd recognized me. Maybe he had amnesia, although this wouldn't explain why he'd told the police that a teenager had attacked him.

When I exited the promenade, my feet were tired and the blister on my foot was starting to bother me again, but I was full of energy. After all the rest I had gotten and with so much on my mind, I knew I wouldn't be able to sleep tonight.

I stopped at the Greek diner at Sixty-fifth and Second and sat at a table in the back. I hadn't eaten all day, but I wasn't hungry. I sipped a cup of coffee and picked at a tuna melt, continuing to contemplate why Rudnick had lied. I must have stayed at the diner for a couple of hours and drunk two refills of coffee, and I could only come up with one likely explanation – he was afraid. He realized that if I was capable of attacking him in a parking lot, then I was capable of anything – including going public with the story of what had happened in his basement. He also knew that if he told the truth and I was arrested, his law career would be finished. It figured that an arrogant fuck like Michael Rudnick would put his job ahead of everything else.

Thanks to the caffeine in my blood, I was even more awake when I left the diner. It was eleven-thirty when I arrived back at the apartment. The lights in the bedroom were off, so I assumed Paula was in bed asleep. I walked Otis, passing the Dumpster where I had thrown out the shopping bag. The Dumpster didn't look like it had been emptied yet, but now I didn't really care. Since there was no investigation going on – at least no investigation involving me – the police wouldn't be searching for any evidence in my neighborhood.

I returned to my apartment and immediately turned on the TV in the living room. On New York 1, there was another report about the stabbing, with some new details. A reporter said that Michael Rudnick had been heading back to his car at approximately eight forty-five yesterday evening, when a white teenaged boy with a ponytail and a goatee approached him, demanding money. Rudnick claimed that he was trying to reason with the teenager when the guy suddenly "went berserk" and attacked him with a knife. Then the reporter gave an update on Rudnick's physical condition. Besides suffering from blood loss, his left lung had collapsed and might have to be removed, and he had suffered severe injuries to his groin area.

I was glad to hear that Rudnick was suffering. I hoped that "severe injuries to his groin area" meant that I had cut off his balls.

I was sitting on the couch, enjoying my new lease of life, when I heard the front door opening. Convinced someone was breaking in, I was on my way to the kitchen, to get the butcher knife, when Paula appeared in the vestibule.

"You scared the shit out of me," I said. "I thought you were asleep."

"Sorry," she said coldly.

"Don't do that again."

"I said I was sorry – Jesus."

"So where were you?"

"Where were *you*?"

"Out," I said. "Walking... and thinking."

"That's where I was – out walking and thinking."

"Look, I'm sorry, all right?" I said. "I've just been going through something – maybe it's alcohol withdrawal. But I'm a new man now – you'll see."

Paula looked at me like I was a stranger.

Finally, she said, "I'll see you in the morning," and headed toward the bedroom.

Although I had spent most of the night awake on the couch, I was up and alert by six-thirty. I tiptoed into the bedroom, careful not to wake Paula, and changed into shorts and a T-shirt and dug out my Nike running sneakers from the back of my closet.

It was a beautiful spring morning – bright sunshine, mild, a gentle breeze. I did some stretching in front of the building, concentrating on my tight hamstring muscles, then I started jogging, slowly, toward Central Park. After a couple of blocks I was winded and I had to walk the rest of the way.

In the park, I jogged along the main road for about a quarter-mile, and then I started gasping for air on an uphill. I also developed stomach cramps and the blisters on my feet were bothering me again even though I'd covered them with layers of Band-Aids. I rested for a while on a grassy area, then I headed home.

My first day of exercise wasn't exactly a major success, but at least it was a start. On Lexington Avenue, I stopped at a deli and bought fruit salad and fat-free cottage cheese. From now on I was going to take care of myself – avoid junk food, join a gym.

I ate breakfast at the dining room table, reading the

Sunday *Times*. The attempted murder in Princeton had made the third page of the Metro section. I couldn't help laughing to myself when I read how the police were speculating that the stabbing may have been related to recent gang violence at a Trenton high school.

I had started reading the rest of the paper when Paula entered the dining room in her nightgown.

'Are you feeling okay?' she asked.

"I'm feeling great. Why?"

"You're eating fruit for breakfast," she said. "You never eat fruit for breakfast."

"I told you – I'm a new man."

She eyed me suspiciously, then she exited to the kitchen.

I realized how odd my rapid mood swing must seem to Paula. Yesterday, her husband was depressed on the couch; today he was acting like Jack LaLanne. She probably thought I was becoming manic-depressive.

For most of the day, Paula did her best to ignore me. She went up to the roof deck to work on her laptop, then she went out shopping.

Meanwhile, I decided to catch up on some work. I dialed in to the network at the office and worked on a couple of proposals that I needed to get out next week. On the internet, I found a listing for an A.A. meeting tomorrow evening in a church on Seventy-ninth Street.

Around four o'clock, I went down to a florist on Second Avenue and bought a bouquet of twenty red, white, and pink roses. When I arrived back at my apartment the light in the foyer was on so I knew Paula was home. I went into the kitchen and saw her standing in front of the open refrigerator. She turned to look at me, showing no reaction to the flowers, and then she took out a bottle of Evian from the fridge.

"These are for you," I said.

"I saw. Thanks."

She poured a glass of water, drank it quickly, then

walked by me, on her way to the bedroom.

"If you feel like going out to dinner tonight –"

"Stop it," she said, turning around suddenly. "All right – just stop it. I didn't move out, but that doesn't mean I'm ready to just pick up where we left off, like nothing happened. You've done a lot of damage and buying me some bullshit flowers isn't going to make things better."

She marched into the bedroom, slamming the door behind her.

On the six o'clock news, I found out that Michael Rudnick was dead. According to the brief news item, his condition had worsened overnight and he had died at around four in the afternoon, at just about the same time I was buying Paula the flowers.

At first, the news upset me, not because Rudnick had died – the world was a better place with one less scumbag in it – but because I had kind of liked the idea of Rudnick living the rest of his life in pain and in fear of me attacking him again. But then, after a while, the news settled in and I decided that Rudnick living for a little over a day, then dying, was probably the best thing that could have happened for me. If Rudnick had died right away, in the parking lot, the police definitely would have questioned me and I might have been arrested. But by setting the police on a wild-goose chase for a teenager, Rudnick had almost guaranteed that I would get away with his murder.

During dinner, Paula still wouldn't speak to me. I tried to start a conversation several times, but she kept looking down at her food, pretending I wasn't there.

Finally, I said, "So I'm going to an A.A. meeting tomorrow night."

"So?" Paula said, still staring at her plate.

"So... so I thought you'd be happy," I said.

She swallowed a bite of chicken chow fun then said, "Well, I'm not."

Monday morning, I headed to work in the windswept rain. On the corner of Forty-eighth and Park, a gust tore apart my umbrella, and I walked the rest of the way, drenched but still cheerful by the time I reached my office.

There was one message on my voicemail – from Don Chaney, the MIS manager who had been disappointed when we couldn't do his web server project last week. Chaney said he had gotten the okay from his CFO on the proposal I'd sent him for the larger, more lucrative project, and that he was going to fax over the signed contract right away. A few minutes later, I went to the fax machine and, sure enough, the signed contract was waiting.

For at least a minute, I stared at the sheet of paper in semi-shock. For months, I had been struggling to make a sale with no success, and now, with zero effort, a deal had fallen right into my lap.

I went into Bob Goldstein's office, where he was sitting at his desk, reading a newspaper.

"Don't you know how to knock?" he said, without looking at me. I dropped the fax in front of him, watching him start to smile as he read it.

"Son of a gun!" He stood up to shake my hand. "See? I knew you had it in you. Congratulations, *mazel tov!* This is really great news – really great. But this is just a start – I want you to keep pumping away. I want two more big sales this week. But I'm proud of you, Richard – I really am proud."

Word of my sale spread quickly around the office. During the next half-hour or so, several people stopped by my cubicle to congratulate me, including Martin Freiden, the CFO, and Alan Wertzberg, the director of marketing.

To see if I had just been lucky, or if I really was back in my old groove again, I called Jim Turner, the guy who had practically thrown Steve and me out of his office last

Monday. If I could close a sale with Jim Turner, I could close a sale with anyone.

Turner's secretary said he was on another call and I said I didn't mind holding. She came back on the line, saying that he was "still on," and I said, "That's all right, I'll wait." Finally, Turner picked up. After I said hello and reminded him who I was I didn't give him a chance to speak. Instead I said:

"Look, I know we didn't have a great meeting the other day, but I wanted to give you a call anyway just to apologize for any false impression of our company you may have gotten, and to ask you to seriously consider our proposal before you make a final decision. I can guarantee you right now that no consulting company in the city can give you the service and reliability that Midtown offers. You can check our references, talk to anybody you want. I'll tell you what – I'll even have a technician come down to your site, just to prove that we have the absolute best staff –"

"Okay."

I held the receiver up to my ear for three solid seconds before I said, "Excuse me?"

"I said okay, I'll give you guys a shot. What do I have to do, sign that quote you gave me?"

Fifteen minutes later I was by the fax machine, holding a signed quote for an eighty-thousand-dollar job from Jim Turner. When news of my second big success of the morning made it around the office, people started gathering around me like I was a sales messiah. Even I was in awe of myself. I imagined being promoted, or moving on to a new, higher- paying job. Paula and I would work out our problems and we'd move with our two children – a boy and a girl – into a huge house, no, an *estate* in Connecticut.

Bob came by my cubicle and rested a hand on my back. He said, "Two for two, you're batting a thousand today, huh? This is incredible – just incredible. You're on a roll, kiddo."

I knew I would be really pushing my luck, but I decided to call another prospect that I had been trying to close for weeks – the CFO at an accounting firm on Seventh Avenue. The proposal had been for a small job, to update the company's Citrix remote-access software, and the last time I talked to him, a couple of weeks ago, he was still reviewing proposals from other consulting firms. Using my same "no-effort" approach, I began my pitch, then he interrupted and said that his budget for the fall just came through and he was going to fax the signed contract over to me right away.

At the first sales job I'd ever had, at an electronics store at a mall near the campus at Buffalo during my senior year, I had once sold three TVs and one stereo in less than a hour. The feeling of closing was so exhilarating that I decided that day that I wanted a career in sales. Since then, I'd closed much bigger sales for much more money, but nothing had ever been as exciting as my first success – until now. Seeing the signed contract in the fax tray gave me a huge head rush, and I wanted to soak up every second of it.

Just about all the employees at Midtown Consulting crowded around my cubicle, including secretaries from other departments who had never seemed to notice me before. Finally, the crowd thinned, but the office was still buzzing with talk of my success and a few more people came by to congratulate me. My mouth was dry from all the talking I'd been doing, so I went to the concession area to buy a can of soda.

"You're so hot I don't want to get too close to you – I might get burned."

I didn't have to turn around to know that Steve Ferguson was behind me.

"Guess so," I said casually.

I retrieved my Pepsi and started to walk away, then I stopped, unable to resist a parting shot.

"Oh, and, by the way," I said, "if you ever need any sales tips, or just want me to go to a meeting with you or listen to your pitch, just stop by and I'd be happy to help you out."

Smiling, I walked away, trying to imagine Steve's expression.

The rest of the day was incredibly hectic. I spent most of the morning setting the start-up dates for three projects, meeting with Recruiting to make sure we had the right personnel in place, and arranging meetings for later in the week for myself with staff at the three companies to discuss various details. I ordered lunch – pastrami on rye with extra pickles – and ate in my cubicle while I worked. I didn't have time to make any additional sales calls and I probably wouldn't have wanted to push my luck anyway. Three for three was good enough for me and I didn't want to do anything that might taint the memory of a perfect day.

I checked my watch, surprised to see that it was a quarter to six. I stopped what I was doing, figuring I'd log on to the network later on from home to continue working, then I dashed down to the street and hailed a cab. I made it to the auditorium of St. Monica's church on East Seventy-ninth Street near First Avenue just as the A.A. meeting was beginning. I sat down in one of the fold-out chairs arranged in a circle and exchanged hellos with the ten or so people who were there. I was extremely uncomfortable. The other "alcoholics" were mostly men – there were two or three women – and, except for one older guy who was wearing a suit, they looked working-class in jeans, sneakers, T-shirts and hooded sweatshirts. I listened as one man – his face and hands were dirty and I figured he was probably a carpenter or a garbage man – talked about how he used to "beat the living shit" out of his son every time he got drunk. Then another guy chimed in about how he once broke his girlfriend's nose in three places. Then one of the women – she seemed like she was fairly new to the group – said that one time, after a night of heavy drinking, she woke up in bed naked next to a strange man and had no idea how she got there. The woman started to cry and other people in the group consoled her.

The leader of the discussion asked me if I had anything to say and I said I was fine "just listening."

A couple of other people shared their experiences of how they were "better people" now that they had quit drinking, then the meeting ended. The man who used to beat up his son came right over to me and offered to be my sponsor. I said, "Maybe," then I left the church alone and headed home.

I knew I didn't belong in A.A., with a bunch of abusive, low-class alcoholics. I definitely didn't have a "drinking problem" – I had just gone through a rough stretch and had used alcohol to help me through it. But I knew that quitting A.A. would upset Paula, so I decided I would keep going to the meetings – for the time being, anyway.

The rain had stopped and it had become a clear, cool night. I walked down Third Avenue with my suit jacket slung over my shoulder, savoring the fumes, the honking cabs, the noise of teenagers yelling, and the aroma of Thai food. I decided that from now on I was going to live my life to the fullest. I was going to work hard at my job, repair and strengthen my marriage, and turn the misery of the past few months into a distant memory.

I turned the corner on Sixty-fourth Street and was approaching my building when I saw, through the glass doors, two serious-looking men in suits standing by the doorman's desk.

13

"Are you the Richard Segal who once lived on Stratford Road in Brooklyn?" the taller of the two men asked.

They had already shown me their badges and explained that they were detectives with the West Windsor Township Police Department in New Jersey. I had no idea where West Windsor was, but I assumed it was somewhere near Princeton. Before answering the tall detective's question, I glanced at the shorter detective, who had a deadpan look, and then over at Raymond, the doorman, who was eavesdropping.

I was trying not to act panicked.

"Yes, that's the street I grew up on," I said. "Why? What's going on?" "We've been trying to track you down since yesterday," the tall man said. "You know how many Richard Segals and R. Segals there are in Manhattan? A lot. And that's only the ones who spell it like you do – s-e-g instead of s-e-i-g or s-i-e-g. But I'm glad we finally found you. By the way, I'm Detective Sergeant Roy Burroughs. This is my partner Detective Jim Freemont."

I took a closer look at Burroughs, getting the sense that he was the hard-ass of the team. He looked like he was in his fifties, about ten years older than Freemont, except he had artificial-looking jet-black hair while Freemont was bald except for messy tufts of curly brown hair around his ears.

"Can you please tell me what this is all about?" I asked.

"Sorry – of course," Burroughs said, his gaze shifting briefly toward Raymond, who was still eavesdropping. "We have some questions to ask you relating to a case we're working on."

"A case?"

"Probably nothing to be concerned about," Burroughs

said ominously. "Do you think we can do this up in your apartment where we might have a little more privacy?"

"Okay," I said. "But can you tell me what kind of case you're talking about?"

"A homicide," Burroughs said.

"A homicide?" I said, trying to act shocked. "Who... What's going on? Is my wife okay?"

"Your wife is fine," Freemont said. "I don't know if you heard, but the man who was killed is someone you once knew. We understand he grew up in a house across the street from you."

"Who?" I asked.

"Michael Rudnick," Burroughs said.

I paused, as if I were letting it soak in. Meanwhile, I was trying to decide how to react. I didn't want to sound totally confused because I knew the police might have found out that I had been to Rudnick's office last Thursday. On the other hand, I didn't want to sound as if the news didn't surprise me, which was easy because I had absolutely no idea how the police had found out that Rudnick had lived across the street from me.

"Wow," I finally said. "That's awful. But I don't get it. Why do you want to talk to me about this?"

"I think we should do this upstairs," Freemont said coldly.

"Why," I said, "what's going on?"

"I really think we should go upstairs," Freemont said.

"Why?" I said. "I don't understand."

A thin, middle-aged, red-haired woman who lived in my building was passing by, overhearing the conversation. I didn't know her name, but I saw her all the time in the elevator and when she was walking her little black pug.

"Fine," I said to the detectives. "Let's go."

In the elevator, riding with the detectives, I said, "You'll see this is a big mistake – I have nothing to do with any of this. And, you know, you guys have *some* nerve, causing a scene like that in my building. What if someone from my co-op board heard you?"

"We suggested going upstairs right away," Freemont said.

"I live here," I continued, ignoring him. "I have to see these people every day. You know, maybe I shouldn't be talking to you at all without a lawyer."

"You're not under arrest," Burroughs said. "But if you think you need a lawyer, we can take you back to the police station in Jersey. It's about an hour-and-a-half drive."

"I didn't say I *need* a lawyer," I said, afraid I was starting to sound guilty. "I don't even understand why you want to talk to me in the first place."

Burroughs looked over at Freemont, who remained staring straight ahead at the elevator doors. As we entered my apartment, Otis started barking venomously, the way he always did when strangers arrived. I asked the detectives to sit down on the living room couch, then I went to lock Otis in my office, noticing that the bedroom door was closed and there was the noise of soft rock music coming from inside, meaning that Paula was home from work. I returned to the living room and sat on the cushioned chair across from the couch where the two detectives were seated.

"So can you please tell me what this is all about?" I said.

"Maybe you should start by telling us what happened last Thursday," Burroughs said accusingly.

"Last Thursday?" I said, as if confused.

"We understand you were in Michael Rudnick's office last Thursday morning," Freemont said.

I glanced toward the balcony, shaking my head, then I looked down at my lap. I let a good ten seconds go by before I said, "Yes – I was in Michael Rudnick's office."

"Did you kill him?" Burroughs asked.

"What's going on here?"

Paula had come out of the bedroom and was standing

to my right. She had changed out of her work clothes into shorts and a T-shirt.

"Nothing," I said. "There just seems to be a big misunderstanding here. These men are detectives from the Jersey police."

"The police?" Paula said. "Why are the –"

"Are you Mr Segal's wife?" Burroughs asked.

"Yes," Paula said.

"Do you mind joining us?"

"Why does she have to be here for this?" I asked.

"What's going on here?" Paula demanded.

"A friend of your husband was murdered," Freemont said.

"He wasn't my friend… He was just an acquaintance. An old acquaintance."

"Who?" Paula asked.

"Michael Rudnick," Burroughs said.

"Who's Michael Rudnick?" Paula asked.

"He's a guy who grew up across the street from me in Brooklyn," I said.

"I never heard you mention him before."

"Maybe you'd like to take a seat and join us, ma'am," Freemont said to Paula.

"Can you please tell me what's going on? Right this instant," Paula said to me.

"I went to see Michael Rudnick last Thursday at his office."

"Why did you go there?"

"Does she really have to be here for this?" I asked the detectives.

"Yes," Burroughs said.

I let out a breath, then said, "I ran into him on the street one day last week and started talking computers with him. He was running some outdated system at his office, so I thought I could sell him an upgrade – you know, get some business out of it."

"Cut the crap," Burroughs said.

"It's the God's honest truth," I said.

"We know why you were there," Freemont said. "We just want to hear it from you – in your own words."

"I still don't understand what any of this has to do with a murder," Paula said.

"It doesn't," I said.

"Tell us what really happened in Rudnick's office," Burroughs said, "or, I don't care, we'll all go to Jersey."

"I told you what happened," I said. "I was trying to sell him a computer network."

"Yeah?" Burroughs said. "And how about how you accused him of molesting you?"

I stared at Burroughs with a blank expression. Then I started to feel queasy, like I was passing out.

"Is that true?"

I had the sense that Paula had asked me this question already, at least once.

"Is it?" she asked impatiently.

I knew I couldn't keep it a secret any longer. Looking down at my lap, I nodded slowly. For about a minute, no one spoke. Paula sat in a chair next to me. Although I was looking down, I sensed everyone watching me, waiting for me to answer.

"Why didn't you tell us this right away?" Burroughs asked.

"Why the hell do you think?" I said, still looking at my lap.

"I wish you'd told me," Paula said coldly.

I looked over at the detectives. "Do you have any other questions to ask me or can you leave us alone now?"

"Don't worry, we'll tell you when we're through," Burroughs said. "Why don't you tell us the whole story now, starting with why you decided to go to Michael Rudnick's office last week and what exactly went on between you two."

I was silent for several seconds, then I told an abbreviated version of how I'd run into Rudnick on the street one day and how, later, I'd started having flashbacks of what he had done to me. I explained how I was just going to forget about the memories at first, but then I decided to go to Rudnick's office to get an apology.

"And when he wouldn't apologize you attacked him," Burroughs said.

"I never attacked him," I said.

"According to Rudnick's wife you did."

"Rudnick's wife?" I said. "What does she have to do with this?"

"On Thursday night, when Rudnick returned home from work, he told his wife how you came to his office that morning, accusing him of molesting you, and how you attacked him."

This explained how the police had known to look for a Richard Segal in Manhattan, but I was surprised Rudnick had told his wife about me. Wouldn't he have wanted to keep me a secret?

"Well, that's not what happened," I said.

I looked over at Paula for support. She was still standing up, her arms crossed in front of her chest now, still seeming semishocked by the whole situation.

"Then why don't you give me your version," Burroughs said.

"I went to his office to talk to him," I said. "He got angry and started screaming at me, and then he tried to hit me. What was I going to do, just stand there? So I pushed him off me, onto his desk, and that's when the maintenance guy or whoever came in to break it up."

Burroughs and Freemont didn't seem convinced.

"Did you know that Michael Rudnick was accused of child molestation once before?" Burroughs said.

I didn't know if this was some kind of trick question.

"No," I said.

"Three years ago," Burroughs said. "A kid on a soccer team Rudnick coached made the accusation. It made the local papers."

I saw myself in the parking lot, coming at Rudnick with the knife.

"What happened?" I asked.

"Kid changed his story," Burroughs said. "No charges were filed."

"So what does this have to do with me?"

"Maybe you heard about what happened with the kid and it caused these 'flashbacks' you had."

"I told you, I know nothing about any kid."

"What time did you come home from work last Friday night?" Burroughs asked.

"Friday night?" I said. "Why Friday night?"

"Just answer the question, please."

I thought quickly. I knew I couldn't tell the detectives the truth, that I came home that night at around ten-thirty. But, with Paula sitting right there, I couldn't lie and say I was home at five or six either.

"I don't know. Late," I said.

"How late?"

"I don't know – nineish," I said, taking a chance that Paula might have forgotten the actual time.

"Where were you before that?" Burroughs asked.

"Drinking," I said.

"Drinking?" Burroughs said as if he didn't believe me.

"Where were you drinking?"

"At a bar," I said.

"What bar?"

"The Old Stand. On Second Avenue."

Freemont was writing in his pad as Burroughs asked me, "When did you get there?"

"I went right after work – around five-thirty, I guess."

"And how long did you stay?"

"Until about eight-thirty or so."

"Were you with anybody?"

"No," I said.

"Is this typical behavior? Drinking alone on a Friday night?"

"Unfortunately, yes," I said, looking at Paula. "I'm an alcoholic."

Paula half-smiled, obviously pleased to hear her husband admit for the first time that he had a drinking problem.

"Can anybody vouch for you?" Freemont asked. "Somebody else in the bar maybe."

"I don't know," I said. "I mean there were a lot of people there. It's possible."

"What about the bartender?" Freemont asked me. "You think he might remember you?"

"Maybe," I said, "but the place was crowded. I really don't know."

"Describe the bartender who served you," Burroughs said.

"I'm not sure who served me."

"Had you been to this bar before?"

"Yes, but they have a lot of bartenders there. I know there's an old Irish guy and a young guy with blond hair and sometimes there's a woman with dark hair there. Actually, I think a combination of people might have served me that night."

"A combination of people," Burroughs said skeptically.

"That's right," I said. "A combination of people."

"Mrs Segal," Burroughs said, turning to Paula.

"Borowski," Paula said.

"Pardon?"

"My last name's Borowski, not Segal. I kept my maiden name."

"I'm sorry – Ms. *Borowski*. When did you see your husband on Friday evening?"

Paula and I made brief eye contact. She shifted

141

uncomfortably then said, "Around the time he said he got home – about nine o'clock."

I blinked slowly, letting out my relief.

"Did your husband seem like he had been drinking?" Burroughs asked.

"Yes," Paula said. "As a matter of fact, he did."

"Did he tell you he had been to the Old Stand?"

"No," Paula said. "But I know he's gone to that bar before. I mean, he's mentioned the name to me."

"Well, I guess we'll just have to look into this ourselves," Burroughs said. Turning back to me, he added, "Do you own any large knives, Mr Segal?"

"Sure," I said. My mouth was suddenly dry. "I mean it depends what you consider large."

"One with at least a four- or five-inch blade."

"Maybe," I said.

"Of course we do," Paula said to me.

"You mind if we take a look in your kitchen?" Burroughs asked.

"No, go right ahead," Paula said.

"Yes, we mind," I said. "You're not looking at anything in this apartment without a search warrant or until I talk to a lawyer. What else do you want?"

Burroughs smiled, and then he stood up. Freemont stood too, closing his notepad.

"I guess there's no use wasting any more of our time," Burroughs said to me. "After all, you have an alibi. We'll just see if any of the bartenders at this bar remember you from Friday night. You'll have to give us a picture of yourself, though, unless you want to come to Jersey and meet our photographer."

"I'll give you a picture," I said.

"I'll get one," Paula said, and headed toward the bedroom.

"A clear one," Burroughs added.

I walked ahead of the detectives, leading them toward

the foyer. From behind me, Burroughs said, "I see you bought the *Times* last Sunday."

I turned around slowly and saw him standing over the basket of newspapers in the corner.

"Yeah," I said, wondering what he was he getting at. "So?"

"Just an observation," Burroughs said. "I noticed the Metro section is on top – that's the section where the story on the stabbing appeared."

"So?"

"So did you read the Metro section or not?"

"I only read the Business section and the Week in Review," I said.

"Me, too," Burroughs said, smiling.

There was awkward silence and I tried to avoid eye contact. Finally, Paula returned with a few photos and said, "Are these any good?" Then she said to me directly, "They're from the Berkshires."

"This one should do," Burroughs said, picking one of me in front of the Red Lion Inn, taken right after we'd checked out.

At the door, Burroughs said to me, "Last question – do you happen to know a teenaged boy with a ponytail and a goatee?"

"No," I said. "Why do you ask that?"

"No reason," he said, smiling again. "We'll definitely be in touch again soon."

When the detectives were gone I said to Paula, "Can you believe this shit? They're really trying to pin a murder on me – a murder."

"Why did they ask if you knew that teenager?"

"I have no idea," I said. "This whole thing is so crazy, like a nightmare. I come back from my first A.A. meeting and next thing I know I'm being accused of murder."

"Want me to make some tea?"

"Whatever," I said.

I went into the bathroom and leaned over the sink, splashing cold water against my face. My mind was spinning but I was finally able to relax. I figured that the detectives would come back after they talked to the bartenders at the Old Stand, but at least I had bought a little more time. What worried me was why the police had decided to question me at all. I didn't know if it was just a routine part of their investigation, or if they knew that Rudnick had lied about the teenager.

Heading back toward the kitchen I heard one of the counter drawers closing. When I entered the kitchen, Paula was trying to look busy, removing dishes from the dishwasher.

"You were looking at the knives, weren't you?" I said.

"No," Paula said. "I was just putting away dishes."

"Please don't lie to me," I said.

She continued to stack dishes for several seconds, then she stopped what she was doing and said, "Why did you pack a suitcase on Saturday?"

"What do you mean?"

"There was a packed suitcase on the bed on Saturday. Were you planning to go somewhere?"

"Yes, I was, actually," I said. "I was thinking about moving to a hotel for a few days."

"Why?"

"Why do you think? You were locking me out of the bedroom – I thought we could use some time apart... What's this all about anyway? You think I killed him, don't you?"

"Of course I don't –"

"Then why are you acting like this?"

"I'm not sure." She looked away for several seconds, covering her eyes, then turned back and said, "Of course I don't think you're a killer, Richard, but things have been so screwed up between us lately I don't know what's going on anymore."

"Look," I said, "everything's gonna be okay. They're gone now and they're not gonna come back."

"Why didn't you tell me?"

"Tell you what?"

The tea kettle started to whistle. Paula turned the flame off and I asked her to make me a cup of Earl Grey. A few minutes later she brought the filled mug to me at the dining room table, then she sat down across from me with her own mugful.

"Maybe the kid's father killed him," I said.

"What are you talking about?" Paula said.

"Rudnick," I said. "The police said the soccer team kid changed his story, but let's say Rudnick really did it. Maybe the father killed him – getting revenge."

"Tell me what happened," Paula said.

"What do you think of my theory?" I said.

"I think it's possible," she said.

She waited, staring at me.

"I really don't remember anything more than I told the detectives," I said. "It happened and it's over and I just want to forget about it."

My hand was gripping the handle of the mug. Paula reached over and put her hand around mine and said, "It wasn't your fault."

"I know," I said.

"Sometimes people tend to blame themselves instead of the other person."

"Believe me, I don't."

"You don't have to feel ashamed –"

"I'm not."

"Or guilty."

"I don't. Really – I'm okay. I mean I understand what you're saying, but it happened a long time ago and it's over now. I guess it's really over since Michael Rudnick's dead."

"You might *think* it's over," Paula said, "but something

like this won't just go away. It might take years until you understand how you really feel."

"I don't need therapy."

"I'm not saying you do –"

"That might work for you, but it won't for me. Believe me, I'm a lot better off just working things out myself. I know it wasn't my fault, that it had nothing to do with me. I know all that crap. Who knows? Maybe if I never remembered what happened, I would've had more problems to deal with. But now I know I'm over it."

"You might not be," Paula said. She let go of my hand and sat up straight. "I'm not going to tell you to see a therapist, so just hear me out, okay? I think therapy would help you, but if you don't want to do it, then don't do it – that's completely up to you. It probably wouldn't help anyway, if you didn't believe in it. But you should definitely open up about your feelings more. If you don't talk to someone about things like this it can cause other problems in your life."

"But isn't that what we're doing now... talking?"

"I mean all the time. From now on we can't just... I mean look at us lately. I can't remember the last time we had a serious talk about anything. We have to be closer. It's not good for two people in a marriage to be acting the way we've been acting. And especially now – with this whole crazy situation with this guy winding up dead. You're going to have a lot of issues coming up – scary issues – and you can't keep them to yourself."

Paula looked down and I realized she'd started to cry. Suddenly, everything made sense. *This* was her "big issue" that she talked about with her therapist, but that she never wanted to discuss with me. It also explained why she used to tell me she always had "trouble getting close to people."

Paula was quiet for a while, then she told me how when she was nine her uncle Jimmy had abused her. Whenever Paula went over to her cousin's house to sleep over, Jimmy would tell her to bring a homework assignment. Then Jimmy would take her into his office, explaining to the other kid that they needed privacy. After Jimmy helped Paula with her homework he would force her to give him a hand job. Paula never told on Jimmy for the usual reasons – guilt, fear, shame – but unlike me, she didn't block out the memories for years. As a teenager, she remembered everything that had happened to her, in vivid detail.

"I'm glad I didn't repress any of it," she said, "or who knows? Maybe I would've become a drug addict or a prostitute. Or maybe I would've gone crazy."

Still, the abuse had a major effect on her. When she was seventeen she started missing her period and her doctor diagnosed her as "borderline anorexic." She had problems dating in high school, going out with verbally, and occasionally physically, abusive guys. When she went away to college she fell in love with me and was convinced that her troubles with relationships were behind her. But then, after we got married, she started feeling bad about herself again.

"I'm not making any excuses," she said. "Cheating on you was stupid and hurtful and it was probably the biggest mistake of my life. But at least I realize why I did it, and I never would have been able to do that without therapy."

She paused and took a sip of tea. I reached over the table and held her hand.

"I'm sorry," I said.

"Don't be," she said. "If I could live my life over I wouldn't change a thing. I've learned that what happened to me with Jimmy is part of who I am. If it wasn't for Uncle Jimmy I'd be a completely different person and I don't want to be a different person – I like myself now."

Thinking that she was even deeper into this therapy crap than I'd thought, I said, "I just wish you'd talked to me about it right away. I could've... I don't know... helped."

"I tried to talk to you about it once," she said, "but I

couldn't. Communication was a big problem for us – it still is a problem. That's why I still need therapy so badly. Except for Dr Carmadie, you're the only person I've ever talked to about any of this."

"Well, it's over now for both of us," I said, starting to massage her hand gently. "Now we can go on with our lives."

She jerked her hand away.

"It's not over for me," she said. "Maybe it's over for you, but it'll never be over for me. I don't mean to belittle what happened to you, but do you really have any idea what I went through? This guy, Michael Rudnick, he wasn't related to you. Can you imagine growing up, having the person who's abusing you in your *family*? Watching your parents treat him like he's this great person when you know he's a scumbag? I don't think anyone can understand what that's like unless it's happened to them. In a way, you were lucky."

"Lucky?"

"Maybe not lucky – *fortunate*. You had a chance to confront Michael Rudnick before he died. I never had that chance. My uncle died a year after he moved to Chicago. Just dropped dead mowing the grass in his backyard one morning. I cried for days when I found out. How fucked up is *that*? I actually cried over that sick fucking bastard. I mean I can really understand why you went to his office that day to confront him. I can't tell you how many times I've fantasized about confronting my uncle. I'd look him in the eye and say, 'Fuck you, you ugly son of a bitch. How could you do that to a child?' Other times, I imagine him sitting there in the reclining chair in his office, in the same chair he used to make me sit in when... Anyway, he's sitting there, smoking one of his stinky cigars, and I sneak up behind him with one of those strings that Mafia guys use. I put the string around his neck and then pull, so hard he gets lifted up off the chair. Then I watch his big bald head turn purple until he stops struggling, until I just let go, and his fat, ugly body falls back onto the chair."

Suddenly, Paula's face was turning bright pink, as if someone were strangling *her*. I could tell that in her mind she was there, killing her uncle, and I remembered how exhilarated I had felt when I was attacking Rudnick in the parking lot, as if for a few seconds I was outside my body, watching myself, the way people are supposed to feel before they die. I felt an urge to tell her the truth about everything. Maybe she'd understand why I'd done it and I wouldn't have to keep it a secret from her anymore.

But instead I said, "I'm glad you didn't do that."

"Why?" Paula asked, her face still flushed.

"Because people might not've believed you. You could've gone to jail, your life ruined because of some fucking pervert."

Paula was crying. I went over and put my arms around her waist. After a while, she put her arms around me and we held each other that way for a long time.

While Paula was getting ready for bed, I walked Otis. Now that Paula and I were back on good terms, there was a noticeable change in Otis's personality. He was much spunkier than he had been lately, walking ahead of me, exploring all the people and objects we passed, keeping the leash taut.

As I walked Otis toward Second Avenue, I realized why Rudnick had told his wife about me. He was afraid I would blackmail him, so he'd told his wife that I had accused him of molesting me *before* I had a chance to make any demands. He'd probably told her that I was crazy and had made up the molestation story to capitalize on what I'd heard about him and the kid on the soccer team. This way, if I took my story public there would be a chance his wife would believe him.

I smiled, thinking about how desperate Rudnick must have been during his last days alive.

At the corner of Sixty-fourth and Second, I considered continuing east and checking on the Dumpster where I had thrown out the bag of evidence. Then I decided this was too risky – for all I knew, the police were watching me, waiting to see if I made a dumb move – so I made a U-turn and headed back toward my building.

14

For the first time in over a week, Paula and I made love. In the morning, when the alarm went off, we were still hugging. I didn't want to get up. It felt too good, having my wife back next to me, where she belonged. I realized how close I had come to losing her and I promised myself that I'd never let anything come between us again.

We showered together. Although we didn't have time to make love again, we kissed and lathered each other all over like newlyweds. We wished that it wasn't a workday or we could call in sick, but we planned to be home early, by seven o'clock, and to spend the whole night together.

Paula had an early meeting and left the apartment at around a quarter to seven. I took my time, shaving and getting dressed. Despite everything that had happened during the past twelve hours, I felt invigorated. I turned on the stereo and listened to a rock station, which was unusual for me. For years, I'd been getting dressed in the morning in silence.

I walked Otis, then I returned to the apartment and had a breakfast of raisin bran, half a glass of orange juice, and a piece of toast. By eight o'clock, I was out the door.

I swiped in at 8:30 on the dot, looking forward to a long day of work. I had the three new projects to coordinate and I was going to be busy all day. I felt like I was a star again, a top performer, the way I used to feel at my old job at Network Strategies. As I walked up the corridor toward my cubicle there was a hop in my step, an inner confidence that had been missing in recent months. I didn't feel like I was just showing up to cash a paycheck anymore. Now I was an important part of the company. I belonged.

I spent most of the early morning on the phone with Jim Turner and other people in the MIS department at Loomis

& Caldwell, discussing the upcoming Linux conversion project. I made an appointment for myself, one of my company's project managers, and a couple of our IT guys to visit the Loomis & Caldwell offices at two o'clock. I was so involved in work that I almost forgot all about the police investigation. Occasionally, I remembered a snippet of dialogue from the detectives' questioning, or wondered if they had talked to the bartenders yet, but I wasn't very concerned anymore. The only reason the police had come to talk to me at all was because I had threatened Rudnick in his office. There was no evidence against me and the best lead was still Rudnick's claim that a teenager had stabbed him. No matter how badly Burroughs wanted to nail me he would have a hard time getting past that one.

At eleven o'clock, I met with Bob Goldstein and two project managers, Alex Petrovsky and Paul Evans, to discuss personnel issues relating to the upcoming projects. When the meeting was over, at around noon, Bob asked me to stick around because he wanted to discuss something "in private."

Sitting across from each other at the conference table, Bob said, "I have some good news for you. This has nothing to do with the sales you made yesterday. We don't make decisions at this company based on one day of success, but it just so happens that Mary in Recruiting resigned yesterday –"

"You're kidding me."

"The news came as a surprise to me, too. Anyway, she'll be gone in a couple of weeks, so you can move into her office. I think it's a little bigger than your old office, so you should be happy there."

Back at my cubicle, I couldn't help laughing to myself. Maybe the new office had developed because Mary had resigned, but if I hadn't had that great day yesterday there was no way Bob would have given me an office. Obviously, Bob felt I'd redeemed myself for my awful sales slump, and if I closed a few more big deals within a couple of months he'd probably promote me to VP of marketing. Steve Ferguson and I were next in line for a promotion, but I knew there was no way Bob would promote a "goy" ahead of a "fellow Jew."

The two o'clock meeting with Jim Turner and his people went extremely well. We discussed the timetable and scheduling for the upcoming job, and compatibility issues relating to the software upgrades. When the main meeting ended I met with Jim in private in his office, schmoozing about a number of different topics, none relating to work. Normally, I would have invited him out for drinks later in the week, or maybe taken him to a strip club, but I knew it would probably be a bad idea to tempt myself with alcohol. Instead, I suggested that we go to a Yankees game sometime in the next week or two. Bob had sets of corporate season tickets to Yankees, Knicks, and Rangers games, for the Midtown salespeople to use to wine-and-dine clients. Jim said that he was a big Yankees fan and that going to a game sounded like a great idea. We talked for a while longer, then we shook hands and he said, "I think this is all going to work out very nicely – I couldn't be happier," before we exchanged goodbyes.

Riding uptown in a cab, I felt upbeat and unstoppable, like I always did after a successful meeting with a client, but then I arrived at the office and I knew right away that something was wrong. Karen usually gave me a big smile whenever I passed by the reception desk, but this time she looked at me strangely. I said hello and she paused, apparently still mesmerized by something, before she said, "Oh, hello, Richard."

In the hallway, I passed Heidi and, in a curt tone, she said, "Bob was looking for you before." Rather than continuing on to my cubicle, I went straight to Bob's office.

Bob was at his desk, working at his PC. Remembering how I'd barged into his office the other day and how annoyed he'd gotten, I knocked on the half-open door. Bob looked over at me and said, "Richard, take a seat."

The chummy tone that he had used earlier in the afternoon was gone. Now he was speaking to me like he had a week or two ago, when my job was on the line.

"Anything wrong?" I asked, sitting down across from him.

"I hope not," he said. He studied me for a few seconds, then he said, "You didn't tell me the police came to your apartment last night."

I looked at him blankly for a moment or two, collecting my thoughts. Then I said, "It really wasn't any big deal."

"Not a big deal? It was about that story that's been all over the news – about that lawyer who was murdered. They said you're a suspect."

"Who said that?"

"The detectives who were here before."

"That's the word they used? *Suspect*?"

"Whatever – they said they were investigating you. They said you went over to the lawyer's office last Thursday afternoon and made a big scene, fighting with him. That was the day you called in sick, when Heidi saw you on Madison Avenue."

"It was all just a big misunderstanding," I said, smiling, trying to make light of the situation. "Yes, I knew the guy who was killed – yes, I was there that day – and yes, we had some *issues* in the past. But I had absolutely nothing to do with whatever happened in New Jersey. I can't even believe the police bothered to come to talk to you about it."

Bob was staring at me seriously. He said, "They didn't just talk to me – they talked to some other people in the office too – and it didn't seem like they were *bothering* with anything. It seems like they're running a serious murder investigation and you're the focus of it."

"That must've just been the impression you got," I said. "I'm telling you, they don't really believe I was involved.

They just wanted to talk to me... as a witness."

"They asked a lot of questions about you," Bob said.

"What kind of questions?"

"Mainly about your whereabouts last Thursday and Friday. I had to have Ricky in Systems give them your swipe-in and swipe-out times on those days. I guess they're trying to put some kind of timeline together."

"I'm sorry this happened," I said. "This whole thing has just gotten way out of control."

"Look, I don't want to get involved in your personal life, all right? Believe me, that's not my intention at all. But when the police come into the office conducting a murder investigation, it becomes my business. I had a client with me. Needless to say, the police were a major distraction."

"I understand," I said. "But I'm telling you – it's just a misunderstanding."

Bob's arms were crossed in front of his chest. "Look," he said, "I guess I just wanted to hear your side, all right? You've obviously been turning things around saleswise. I hope, for your sake, this police investigation turns into nothing."

Leaving Bob's office, I noticed that people were avoiding me. If everyone in the office didn't already know that I was a murder suspect, it was only a matter of time before they did.

I decided not to let the situation depress me. Instead, I returned to my cubicle and focused on work. Unlike yesterday, when I was the big hero in the office and people were coming over to congratulate me almost nonstop, everyone kept their distance. At one point, I looked up and saw Steve Ferguson talking to Rob Cohen, the junior salesman, in the hallway, about ten yards away from my cubicle. Steve kept glancing in my direction, smirking, obviously amused by the gossip he had heard about me. I shot him a look that said "Go fuck yourself" and returned my attention to my computer screen.

I knew that the best way I could shut up Steve Ferguson was to make another big sale and that was exactly what I did on my very next call – closing a proposal on a hardware rollout and a network upgrade for 110 users. At the end of the day, when the signed quote came in, I made a copy of the quote and slipped it under Steve's door – a not-exactly-passive-aggressive way of saying "fuck you."

Walking home, with my suit jacket slung over one shoulder, I was enjoying the cool, comfortable evening. Waiting for a light to change on the corner of Fifth Avenue and Forty-eighth Street, I realized that I was on the exact corner where I had spotted Michael Rudnick about two weeks ago. Staring into the crowd waiting to cross the avenue, it was a relief to know I would never have to see his face again.

Approaching my building, I spotted Paula getting out of a cab. We kissed on the sidewalk and then walked inside holding hands. Paula told me all about her day and I told her about mine. When I mentioned how the detectives had spoken to Bob and other people in the office, she became extremely upset.

"You should call a lawyer," she said. "They're harassing you now – it's disgusting."

"I'll think about it," I said.

"Why wouldn't you call a lawyer? What do you have to lose?"

"Nothing, I guess. But the police probably know they don't have a case against me – maybe this is the end of it."

We showered together and then got dressed to go out. Paula put on a black dress and high heels and I wore a sport jacket and a pair of slacks. We went to a Malaysian restaurant on Third Avenue that we had avoided in the past because the menu was too pricey. Now that I was closing sales again, a hundred bucks for a dinner for two was chump change.

After dinner, we went to a cafe on Fifty-ninth Street and shared a piece of opera cake and drank cappuccinos. On the way home, we stopped every so often and kissed. Nearing our block, it started to rain and we jogged the rest of the way, holding hands and laughing.

During the next few days, my life continued to improve. At work on Wednesday a few people went out of their way to be nice to me. Martin Freiden, the CFO, came by my cubicle and said he'd heard about what had happened with the police, and told me that if there was anything he could do to help me I should just stop by his office to ask him. I knew it wasn't a real invitation, that he didn't really want to help me, nor did he really expect me to come to him for advice, but I still appreciated the gesture. Later on, Joe from Marketing, who I was more friendly with, asked me if I wanted to go to lunch with him. I told him that I'd have to take a rain check, that I was too busy, but that I definitely appreciated the offer.

There was no mention of the murder in the Wednesday newspapers. This came as a big relief because I was ready to see the headline SALES EXEC SAYS DEAD MAN MOLESTED HIM. During lunch, I went to an internet cafe in midtown, signing in with a phony name. I did searches on several news sites, but I found only the archived stories from last weekend. The story definitely seemed to be fading and I hoped that this meant the police investigation was fading too.

Still, on the way back to my office, I couldn't help feeling that undercover cops were watching me. I didn't see anyone suspicious and I knew that I was probably just being paranoid, but I looked back over my shoulder every now and then anyway, expecting to see someone duck into a vestibule or look away suddenly.

Paula had still been bugging me about consulting with a lawyer, so I decided to do it, mainly to get her off my back. The lawyer who had handled the closing on our co-op recommended a defense attorney, Kevin Schultz. I called Schultz that afternoon from my office. I explained to him what I had told the police – that I had confronted Rudnick in his office, but that I had absolutely nothing to do with the murder. Schultz said that it didn't sound like I had said anything to incriminate myself, but he urged me not to talk to the police again without his presence.

At six o'clock, I attended my second A.A. meeting. I wasn't planning to speak, but for some reason, when my turn came, I was in the mood to open up. I went on about my experiences with alcohol, talking about how it had all started when I was thirteen, and escalated as I got older. Then I talked about my problems with alcohol lately, how I had hurt my wife while I was drunk, which had been the worst, most regrettable thing I had ever done. My eyes began to tear and I couldn't speak anymore. As I sat back down, everyone applauded.

Paula had picked up groceries on her way home from work and she cooked her specialty – chicken piccata with wild rice and pine nuts. We ate by candlelight, listening to a CD of classical masterpieces, talking almost nonstop. I told her about how, after my parents' divorce, I had felt very lonely. My mother and I had moved to Manhattan when I was in ninth grade and I had to transfer to a junior high school where I didn't know anybody. A few cruel, popular boys started picking on me, calling me "faggot" and "homo." I was beaten up several times and I had no friends. Because my grades in junior high school were poor I couldn't get into Stuyvesant High School and my mother was disappointed in me.

Paula shared more stories from her life. She told me about the time when she was fourteen and she and a friend had tried some cocaine they found in her friend's brother's bedroom. Her friend had a heart attack and nearly died. When Paula was fifteen, shortly after her uncle Jimmy died, she had her own brush with death. Hopelessly

158

depressed, she got in her parents' car, which was parked in an unventilated garage, and turned on the engine. She had started to pass out when her sister discovered her and dragged her to safety. Afterwards, her parents sent her for a psychiatric evaluation. She talked about everything with a psychiatrist except "the big thing," fearing that it would put her parents through too much pain if they found out about Uncle Jimmy. She was prescribed antidepressants, but she continued to suffer from self-loathing and worthlessness.

Then, sounding suddenly serious and foreboding, Paula told me that there was something else she wanted to tell me about her teenage years. Paula had the habit of making trivial issues sound overimportant. One time she had told me that there was something "very serious" she wanted to discuss with me and I braced myself, fearing that a relative had died or had been in a horrible accident, but then she said, "I'm thinking about getting my hair cut." So now I was expecting her to tell me some lighthearted story about her sweet sixteen party or her prom night, but unfortunately this wasn't the case.

I'd always assumed that Paula had been with about ten guys before she met me, which wouldn't have been a big deal, but I was way off. Paula rattled off the names of about twenty boys she'd had sex with in junior high school and high school and she assured me that there were "dozens" of others whose names she couldn't remember. Two of the "unknowns" were the guitar player of an opening band at a Who concert she had attended when she was sixteen, and "some forty-year-old guy" she had met at a roller rink when she was in junior high school. Her only serious teenage relationship was with Andy Connelly – she referred to him as "you know who" – during her senior year of high school. In college, where I had met her, she had "reinvented" herself as a girl with limited sexual experience.

If Paula had broken this news to me a few days ago, I probably would have gotten very upset – after all, finding out that your wife had been a teenage slut, when you had a completely different image of her, is not the most pleasant news a husband can receive – but now I felt nothing but sympathy for her. It was as if there was suddenly an even greater bond between us. We had both been abused as children and had responded to it in different ways – I had lashed out against the person who had hurt me, and she had lashed out against herself.

Later, after we made love, Paula started to cry against my shoulder. I asked her what was wrong, but she insisted it was nothing. Finally, she told me that maybe it was hormones, or maybe it was because she was so happy.

On Thursday, two of my projects got under way. After checking in at each site and meeting with the various coordinators, I returned to my office, where I had internal meetings with project managers and people from Purchasing. Although I was working hard, I didn't feel at all exhausted or stressed.

After work, I joined a health club near my office. I had brought gym clothes with me from home and I spent about twenty minutes on a LifeCycle machine, and then I did a couple of sets of bench presses and pulldowns. I was full of energy and I could have worked out longer, but I didn't want to push myself too hard on the first day. From now on, I planned to work out at least several days a week, during my lunch hour, and on weekends at the health club's Upper East Side location. My goal was to lose fifteen pounds by August. Of course, this meant I wouldn't fit into my old clothes and I'd have to go shopping for a new wardrobe. All the clothes I owned now were plain and conservative, mostly from Today's Man. I needed a sharper, hipper look. Maybe I'd start shopping at Barney's or at boutiques on Madison Avenue.

Paula had told me that she wasn't going to be home until

around eight o'clock, because she had an appointment with her therapist, so I decided to surprise her by cooking dinner. I printed out a recipe for chateaubriand from the internet, and I went to the gourmet food market down the block and bought all the ingredients. I was an awful cook, but I figured that I couldn't screw up too badly with a recipe. When Paula came home the apartment was filled with smoke and the loud, shrill smoke alarm was going off. When she came into the kitchen and saw the charred meat we both had a good laugh.

We threw the food away and ordered in Vietnamese. Afterwards, we walked Otis. It was a warm night, and we were both wearing shorts, T-shirts, and sandals. On First Avenue, we bought Tasti D-Lite cones and ate them on a bench outside the store. We talked, taking breaks to kiss or to just look into each other's eyes.

On the way home, Paula told me how she'd called Dr Lewis today and canceled our upcoming marriage counseling appointment. Now that we had been getting along so well together, Paula didn't think we needed counseling.

Later, while we were washing up, getting ready for bed, Paula told me that she wanted to have a baby. At first I thought she was joking, but then I realized that this wasn't something she would kid about. She thought that maybe it had to do with her sister giving birth last week or because – as her therapist had suggested – she had finally decided what was really important to her in life, but she wanted to go off the pill right away. I hugged and kissed her and I told her how thrilled I was. Then she said she agreed with me, that a child needs a backyard, like she'd had in Syracuse, and we decided that we would start taking trips to Tarrytown and other small towns along the Hudson to start house-hunting, maybe as soon as this weekend.

Paula said she was too tired to make love, so she went to sleep and I stayed up, watching TV in bed, switching back and forth between the various newscasts. Like the past few nights, there was no mention of the murder, and I was becoming increasingly convinced that the case had been forgotten. Within the next few months, Paula and I would find a house in a small, friendly community in Westchester. In the meantime, we'd call a real estate agent and start showing our apartment. Now that my job wasn't on the line and I was on track to start making some decent money in commissions, it didn't matter if we had to take a loss on the apartment. It would be a relief to get out of Manhattan. Maybe I'd miss the energy of the city, but I was sick and tired of living on top of people in an apartment building, sneering at my neighbors in the elevator and not knowing, or wanting to know, their names. I wanted a calm, relaxing, suburban life. I'd ride to work every morning on a commuter train, working on a laptop and sipping a cup of coffee. At work, I'd make a ton of money and I'd have a corner office and I'd be treated with respect by everyone. Then I'd return home and eat dinner with my family. If we had a son, I'd be friends with him, not a stranger like my father was to me. I'd spend time with him in the evenings and on weekends – helping him with his homework and taking him to ball games. Maybe I'd even become the coach of his Little League team.

I turned off the TV and hugged Paula from behind, continuing to envision my bright future. I saw images of us with our two children, sitting around the dinner table, laughing. Then I saw myself and my son, playing catch in the backyard on a bright, sunny day. Then a vision of our whole family appeared – we were standing on a manicured lawn, in front of a lavish house, as if posing for a picture. I was in great shape and I looked like I was twenty-five years old. I had a bronze tan and I was smiling widely.

Then, as I started to fall asleep, my thoughts and dreams merged, and my happy visions faded. The perfect house in the suburbs vanished and so did the children. Now it was just Paula and me alone in our dark, bleak apartment. I saw images of us fighting and heard us screaming at each other. I was calling her "bitch" and "whore," and I was drunk, beating her, and she was crying, and both of her eyes were black and swollen. Then I was running along dark train tracks, holding a bloody butcher knife. It was windy and bitterly cold.

15

I was happy to see the warm pot of coffee in the kitchen. Thanks to a horrible night's sleep, I had a dull headache and I felt extremely weak. I poured myself some coffee, added some skim milk, and took a few sips. Usually, caffeine gave me instant energy, but this morning it had no effect at all.

Paula was still in the shower when I got back into bed to get another five minutes of rest. I must have dozed off, because when I opened my eyes, Paula was dressed, ready to leave. She was in a lousy mood too, so we didn't talk much. She kissed me goodbye quickly before she left.

At work, I still felt lethargic. A crisis at Don Chaney's site – he was unhappy with one of our consultants – distracted me for a while, but it was hard to ignore how miserable I felt. In a cabinet in the kitchen area of the office I found a bottle of Advil. I downed two caplets with some lukewarm coffee. My headache subsided, but the caffeine from all the coffee I'd had on an empty stomach made me extremely anxious. I went down to a cart on the street and bought a bagel and cream cheese, devouring it in several bites on my way back to the office. The food energized me for the rest of the morning, but by noon I was feeling fragile again.

Bob and Alan, the director of marketing, stopped by my cubicle and asked me if I wanted to have lunch with them. Bob had never invited me to have lunch with him before and the gesture was even more unexpected given how he had acted after the police came to the office. Alan was about Bob's age, around forty, and although we always said hello and exchanged pleasantries in the hallway, he had never seemed very interested in me.

We went to a kosher Italian restaurant on Forty-sixth Street. The food sucked, but the conversation was pleasant.

Bob told some of his old Polish jokes and then Alan talked about how his oldest daughter was going off to college at SUNY Buffalo. When I told him I had gone to college at Buffalo there was an immediate bond between us. I gave him my opinions about the campus and the city, telling him that Buffalo was a "great place to spend four years." Although I really thought the entire city was a hellhole, I figured that since his daughter had already made a commitment to the school he wouldn't want to hear anything negative. Later, Alan asked me what my plans were for the future. I was taken aback at first, unsure what he was getting at, and then I said that I wanted to make as much money for the company as possible and take it from there. "Good answer," Bob said, and we all laughed. Then Alan asked me if I had any interest in getting involved in the "marketing side of the business." I said that I'd be interested in any opportunity that was offered to me. Alan said he couldn't make any guarantees, but that a marketing position could be opening soon and that he'd keep me at the top of his list.

We sat at the table, schmoozing, for a long time after the check arrived. On the way back up to the office, in the lobby, we ran into Steve Ferguson. Steve made small talk and tried to act as if nothing was wrong, but the way he refused to even make eye contact with me was a dead giveaway that he was pissed off. I could almost hear his shallow, petty mind pleading, Why are you taking *him* to lunch? What about me? Don't I get any respect at this company anymore?

My future was looking very bright again. If I was promoted to a high-level marketing position, that would put me on track to become a vice president someday, if not at Midtown then at some other networking company. I would make a big guaranteed salary, at least equal to what I was making now, without the pressure of having to close sales.

I called Paula at her office, to tell her the good news, but

I got her voicemail. I left a short message saying, "I just wanted to tell you how much I love you and I miss you very much."

After I hung up there was a short beep on my PC, announcing that I had received an email. Still smiling, thinking about Paula, I opened my email log and saw the strange address of the incoming message:

you_are_a_liar@yahoo.com

A sick feeling was building in my stomach. There was no subject heading and I had no idea who had sent it. Hoping it was just spam, I opened the message.

CONFESS!

For about a minute, I stared at the single word on the screen in front of me, unable to think. Then I forced myself to concentrate, trying to figure out who could have written to me.

I looked at the address again: you_are_a_liar@yahoo. com. Anyone could start a Yahoo email account for free, so the address in itself didn't give any clues. I checked Yahoo to see if there was a profile for this email account but, not surprisingly, there was none. I knew there were ways to trace email addresses. I considered getting help from Chris, one of the web gurus in the office, who often bragged how he had once hacked into Microsoft's system, but I decided that it would be a bad idea to get anyone else involved.

It was getting harder to stay calm. I thought about that night at the train station, wondering if it was possible that someone had witnessed the murder. It didn't make any sense to me why a witness would be telling me to confess, but I didn't know why anyone else would have sent the message either.

I went to the front desk where Karen was sitting, wearing her headset.

"I was just wondering," I said, "did someone, by any

chance, call yesterday or today, asking for my email address?"

"Not today," she said. "But I was out sick yesterday and a temp was here. Someone could have called then."

"Thanks anyway," I said.

I returned to my cubicle. Staring at the message again, I thought about sending a reply. I was about to do it when I decided it could be a big mistake. It was important to show that I was strong, that I wasn't afraid or even concerned. Then a few seconds later, opening my jacket and looking at my sweat-stained shirt, I realized how impossible this was going to be.

On the way home from work, as hard as I tried to act as if it were just a normal Friday, I couldn't stop looking over my shoulder. At one point, I was so convinced that this guy with red hair was following me that I stopped and waited for him to pass by before I turned the corner and continued on. Then, a few minutes later, I became convinced that a black Volkswagen bug was trailing me. I remembered seeing a black bug near Fifth Avenue and now there was one double-parked on Park. I had no way of knowing whether it was the same car or not, but I decided to hail a cab anyway. The bug followed the cab for a few blocks, but when the cab turned right on Sixty-fourth Street, the bug stayed on Park.

Paula was lying on the couch in the living room, listening to one of her old George Michael CDs, reading a magazine. I kissed her hello.

"Sorry I was so nasty this morning," she said. "I'm feeling a lot better now."

I told her I was still feeling "under it" and that I needed to lie down.

I changed into sweatpants and a T-shirt and got into bed. I tried to relax, but I couldn't stop obsessing about the email.

Paula came into the bedroom and lay next to me. She kissed me lightly on the forehead then said, "How are you feeling?"

"Little better," I lied.

"Good," she said. "I'm glad."

She started telling me about her day at the office, about a new project she was working on. I was barely listening, but I kept the conversation going by saying "right" and "really" and "okay" at the appropriate times.

Then, in a suddenly sexy voice, Paula said, "We can start trying next week."

"Trying?" I said, distracted. "Trying for what?"

"To have a baby," she said.

"Sorry," I said, "I forgot. Not *forgot* – I just didn't hear what you said."

"What's wrong?"

"Nothing. A long day, that's all."

Paula hugged me and we were both silent. I felt awful for keeping secrets from her. I wanted to tell her the truth about everything, including the murder. If she loved me as much as I thought she did, then she'd understand.

"It's not true," I said, aware of my face suddenly getting hot.

"What isn't true?" she asked.

"It wasn't just a long day at work – something happened today. Something important."

"What?"

I hesitated.

"Well?" she asked.

"I was sort of offered a promotion," I said, and then I told her about my lunch with Bob and Alan. She told me how proud she was of me, and she suggested taking me out to dinner to celebrate. I said I wasn't really in the mood to go out tonight and, besides, there really wasn't anything to celebrate yet.

Friday evening we stayed in, watching a movie on pay-per-view. I couldn't concentrate on the plot and I fell asleep halfway through. During the night, I woke up several times, imagining the publicity the story would get. The media loved it when ordinary men like me were exposed as killers. It could even become a national news story and I imagined my parents finding out about it. My father was so self-absorbed he'd probably be upset for a few days and then forget about it altogether. But my mother would be devastated. She would probably spend the rest of her life in church, begging Jesus for forgiveness.

On Saturday, Paula went to Bloomingdale's and I went to the gym. I had no energy to lift weights so I spent a few minutes doing ab exercises. Then I went into the sauna, hoping to relax. Unfortunately, sweating only made me more tense, and afterwards my skin itched all over.

On my way home, walking down Second Avenue, I saw a black Volkswagen bug double-parked across the street. The driver was a man with red hair. I remembered how yesterday I had thought that a red-haired man walking behind me was an undercover cop. I couldn't tell if this was the same man or not, but he looked similar enough. I stopped and stared at him, but he didn't look in my direction. Another man came out of a pizza place, holding a pizza box, and got into the car. The red-haired man drove off.

That night, I decided I needed to get out of the apartment, so Paula and I went out to dinner at a Mexican restaurant. When we came home, the phone was ringing. I answered it, but there was no one there. I realized how the same thing had happened a couple of times during the past week. I asked Paula if she'd gotten any hang-ups and she said, "Maybe one or two." I wondered if the calls could have been related to the emails. When Paula went into the bedroom I took the portable phone into the dining room and dialed *69, to automatically call the person who'd phoned last. A Puerto Rican-sounding woman answered,

"Allo," and I hung up, feeling like an idiot.

The next day, Sunday, Paula and I rented a car and drove to Westchester. We drove around through the quaint small towns of Scarborough and Harmon, several miles above Tarrytown on the Hudson. Then, just for the hell of it, we stopped at a real estate office and the agent took us to see a few houses. They were all big and spacious with large bedrooms and big backyards. One of the houses was eerily similar to the perfect suburban home that I had fantasized about living in someday. It was sad, walking around the house with Paula, talking about which would be the baby's room and where the dining room table would go, knowing that I was probably going to prison. I regretted that I had agreed to look at houses in the first place.

Riding back toward the city along the Henry Hudson Parkway, approaching the George Washington Bridge, I looked in the rearview mirror and spotted a black Volkswagen bug. It was hard to tell for sure, but the driver seemed to have red hair.

"Did you notice that car before?" I asked.

"Which car?"

"The one behind us – the black bug."

Paula turned around to look then said, "No. Why?"

"Never mind," I said.

I slowed down until the bug angled to the left lane and passed me. I looked over at the driver – a woman with dirty blond hair – and she glanced at me briefly and then looked back at the road.

I imagined Michael Rudnick laughing, the same way he used to laugh when he was chasing me around the Ping-Pong table.

After we returned the car I walked Otis. It was a warm, oppressive night. Back home, I took a long shower. With the ice-cold water beating down on my head, I had a brainstorm.

16

The next morning at nine o'clock, I burst into Steve Ferguson's office and shouted, "Son of a bitch!"

"What the hell?" Steve said as if he didn't know what was going on. He was at his desk, sipping a cup of coffee.

"Look, I know it was you and it's not going to work," I said, "so you might as well admit it."

He started to smile, in that slick, phony way.

"You're gonna have to slow down, Richie," he said, "because I'm still on my first cup of coffee here and –"

I moved closer to his desk and swatted away some papers to show him how serious I was.

"Hey," he said, standing up to face me, "what the hell's the matter with you?"

"I don't appreciate your pranks," I said, my *P*s spraying saliva. "Maybe you think we have a little rivalry going here and if you can distract me I'll stop making sales and then maybe Bob and Alan will promote you before me. Well, it's not gonna work, no matter how many emails you send me."

Now he wasn't smiling anymore.

"Emails? What the... Are you fucking crazy or something?"

I left his office, slamming the door hard. I dropped off my briefcase by my cubicle, then I went into the bathroom. Staring at myself in the mirror above the sink, I noticed the deep bags under my eyes.

At my desk, I booted up my computer and checked my email log. I had four new messages – three work-related and one from you_are_a_liar.

WE'RE STILL WAITING, ASSHOLE. DON'T THINK YOU'RE GONNA GET AWAY WITH THIS, YOU

JERK-OFF, BECAUSE YOU'RE NOT. YOU HAVE NO FUCKING CHANCE.

The message had been sent at 9:29 last night. I read the note again and again, searching for clues. The grammar wasn't great and I had a feeling the sender wasn't very intelligent. I started focusing on "WE'RE," wondering if more than one person had written to me.

Steve still could have sent the message, but I realized I had probably made a big mistake blaming him. Would he really go to all this trouble just to drive me crazy?

Figuring I had nothing to lose, I decided to send a reply. I thought it over for a couple of seconds, then I typed:

Who are you? I think you might have the wrong guy.

Then, after giving it some more thought, I deleted this and typed:

Sorry, wrong email.

Perfect. I sounded casual and distracted, as if I were too busy to be concerned by some crank emails. I read my note several times, liking it even more, then clicked SEND.

I started working on some new hardware quotes that Jim Turner had requested, but it was hard to stay focused.

Then, at about eleven-thirty, my phone rang.

"You didn't think we forgot about you, did you?" Detective Burroughs asked.

"What do you want?" I asked, wondering if the call had something to do with the email I'd sent.

"I'm afraid we're going to need you here at the police station this afternoon," Burroughs said.

"What for?" I asked.

"We need you to appear in a line-up."

"A line-up?" I said, trying to stay calm. "What for?"

"A witness came forward and we want to see if he can ID you."

"Look, I'm very busy today and –"

"This isn't optional," Burroughs said. "A car's already on its way to your office to pick you up. I was just calling to make sure you were in today."

I thought about calling Kevin Schultz, the lawyer I had spoken to on the phone, but I decided that this would be a bad idea. Demanding to have a lawyer present would only make me seem guilty, as if I had something to hide. It would be better to wait and see if I was really in trouble before calling Schultz. Besides, no lawyer, no matter how good, could stop a witness from identifying me.

"You'll see, you're making a big mistake," I said, "but if you want me to be in a line-up, I'll be in a line-up."

Bob was busy in a meeting and I knew I couldn't just disappear for the day with no explanation. I remembered that one of my new clients, Ken Hanson from the accounting firm on Seventh Avenue, said he was going to be out of town all this week, so I added a bogus 12:30 meeting with him to my Lotus Notes appointment program.

As Burroughs had promised, at noon a police car was waiting for me in front of the office building. It was a nice day and the street was crowded with people going to lunch. I looked around carefully, trying to make sure no one from my office was watching, then I entered the back of the car quickly. I kept my head down until the car pulled away.

The driver – a young, blond officer – didn't say anything when I got in. Jazz was playing on the stereo at a low volume.

Sitting in the back of a police car, on my way to a line-up, probably should have made me nervous, but I was surprisingly calm.

There was hardly any traffic and we made it to the police station in central Jersey in a little over an hour. I expected Burroughs to be waiting for me, but he wasn't there. I was led into a waiting area where two other men were seated. One of them looked drunk and homeless, the other one was a typical New Jersey hick, with a ripped denim jacket, an unruly goatee, and a chewed-up toothpick dangling from the corner of his mouth.

We sat there for at least fifteen minutes. I was getting impatient. Finally, a female officer told us to take off our jackets. She asked me if I had on anything under my shirt. I told her I was wearing a T-shirt and then she told me to take off my tie and dress shirt as well.

The officer led us into a room where two other men in T-shirts were waiting. One of the men looked sixty, and one of them looked like he was twenty. The only thing that all five of us had in common, as far as I could tell, was that we were all white. I was the only one who looked like I worked for a living and like I didn't have some kind of disease.

The officer asked us to line up, with our hands by our sides, in front of a large mirror. She told us to try to maintain a "natural expression," and to keep our heads straight and eyes open.

After about thirty seconds, the officer returned with five pairs of sunglasses. They weren't similar to the pair I'd been wearing the night of the murder, but it was frightening that the police knew about this.

"Now we'd like you to put these on and stare straight ahead again," the officer said.

I put on the sunglasses – they were slightly small on me – and tried to maintain a "natural expression." After about a minute, the officer returned and said, "That's all," and she led us out of the room.

I put on my shirt, tie, and jacket. The other guys were talking to one another, but I kept to myself. A man in a suit – he looked like a detective, but I had never seen him before – came into the room and asked me to come with him.

As I followed the man down the hallway, I wondered if this was it. Somehow, the prospect of getting caught seemed realer now than it ever had before. I imagined myself falling to the floor and crying like a baby when they told me I was under arrest.

The man led me into an interrogation room where Detectives Burroughs and Freemont were seated at a table. Burroughs told me to take a seat, but I remained standing.

"So what's going on?" I asked, trying to prepare for the worst.

"Just sit down," Burroughs said.

"Did your witness ID me or not?"

"Sit down, Mr Segal."

I hesitated for a few seconds, then I sat.

"To answer your question," Burroughs said, "no, the witness couldn't ID you."

"So then take me back to Manhattan."

"I'm afraid that doesn't mean you're off the hook," Burroughs said. "We know you lied to us about your alibi."

"What are you talking about?"

"The Old Stand bar has video surveillance cameras. We looked at the footage and we know you weren't at the bar that night."

I sensed a trick.

"There has to be some mistake," I said, "because I was there that night. I'm telling you the truth."

"Oh, there's no mistake," Burroughs said. "We looked over that tape carefully and there's no doubt about it – you weren't there. So you want to tell us what really happened that night?"

"I told you where I was," I said. "I really don't understand this. Did you talk to the bartenders?"

"Yes, as a matter of fact we did," Burroughs said.

"So? Did any of them recognize me?"

"Two of them did," Burroughs said. "They said you'd come in a few times over the past few weeks, but they couldn't say for sure whether you were there that night."

"That's not my problem."

"Oh, it *is* your problem," Burroughs said, "because we know for a fact you weren't in that bar."

"But I *was* in the bar," I insisted.

"Look," Burroughs said, "we could do this one of two ways. You could admit you killed Michael Rudnick and maybe you'll get a lighter sentence. Or you could make things more complicated for us and you'll get life. It's all up to you."

"This is ridiculous," I said. "You come to my apartment and cause a big scene and embarrass me in front of my wife. Then you show up at my office and cause more embarrassment. And now you drag me out to butt-fuck New Jersey for some pointless line-up when I had a very busy day scheduled. Meanwhile, there is absolutely no evidence that I had anything to do with any of this. You know, I think I'll call a lawyer after all and start talking about a lawsuit. I also have a feeling the local newspapers will want to hear about how your department harasses innocent people."

"Michael Rudnick's penis had been nearly severed," Burroughs said matter-of-factly.

"So?" I said. "What does that have to do with anything?"

"Trying to cut off a man's penis isn't the normal way to kill someone," Burroughs said. "Unless of course the killer was molested by the victim."

"I told you, I was at a bar that night."

"Then how do you explain why you're not on the bar's videotape?"

"Because there is no videotape," I said. "You're trying to set me up when I had nothing to do with any of this."

For about twenty minutes, Burroughs and Freemont took turns grilling me. They tried to poke a hole in my alibi, make me admit that I wasn't at the Old Stand on that Friday night. They had found out that I had scheduled the bogus four o'clock appointment on my calendar that afternoon and I explained that scheduling the appointment had been "an honest mistake." They made me repeat the information I had told them the other night, about the times I had left work, been at the bar, and arrived home at my apartment. I stuck to my story entirely and I could tell that I was wearing the detectives out. Finally, they realized that with no solid evidence against me they couldn't keep me any longer. Burroughs led me back to the front of the precinct and said I would be taken back to Manhattan "as soon as a car is available."

I had to wait over an hour. This gave me plenty of time to think about who the witness could have been. Burroughs had said that "the platform was darkly lit," so the witness must have seen me either when I got off the train at Princeton Junction, or before I got on the train to New York. Burroughs had referred to the witness as a "he," so this ruled out the woman on the opposite platform who had smiled at me. I remembered passing a man in a business suit on the stairs leading up to the platform, then several people who were seated on a bench. One of these people could have been the witness, but I decided it didn't really matter. Some guy might have seen me on the platform that night, but he couldn't have gotten a good look at me or he would have told the cops about my blond hair.

Escaping from my thoughts, I glanced to my right and saw Michael Rudnick standing by the doorway. He looked the way he did as a teenager – overweight, with a faceful of acne and a thick caterpillar eyebrow.

I closed my eyes tightly and when I opened them Rudnick was gone.

17

The elevator doors opened and Bob was facing me. It was past five o'clock and he was holding his briefcase, leaving for the day.

"Where have you been?" he said. "We had a sales meeting at four."

"Sorry," I said. "My twelve-thirty ran late."

"Sure, sure, whatever," he mumbled. "See you tomorrow."

I continued into the office, wondering if I was on Bob's shit list again. Then I decided it didn't matter one way or the other. Maybe a couple of weeks ago he would have threatened my job for scheduling a bogus appointment, but now that I was well on my way to becoming the company's top salesman he was liable to cut me a little more slack.

It was a relief to see that I had received no new threatening emails. I hoped this was a sign that my troubles were over.

I stayed late at the office, trying to catch up on some of the work I had been neglecting lately. Around eight o'clock, I decided to call it a day. I was exhausted and it was another humid, oppressive night, so I took a cab home.

Paula greeted me at the front door. She said she was worried about me, but then remembered that I'd had an A.A. meeting tonight. I had completely forgotten about the meeting, but I covered for myself smoothly. I told her that the meeting had gone "very well." She asked me what we'd talked about and I said, "You know, the usual – our experiences drinking, sharing stories." Paula said, "I'm so proud of you," and then she said there was warm Chinese food waiting for me in the kitchen.

I ate some shrimp with snow peas, although I wasn't very hungry. I opened my fortune cookie and read the fortune out loud to Paula: "You are in charge of your destiny."

"That probably had to do with your A.A. meeting tonight," she said.

"Probably," I said.

Paula and I sat on the couch together watching TV. I was starting to fall asleep when the phone rang. Paula said she'd get it, but I was closer to the phone so I answered it. I said, "Hello," but the person hung up right away.

"Who was it?" Paula asked.

"Another wrong number," I said. "If this keeps happening I'll have to call the phone company."

I returned to the couch and fell right asleep.

> THIS IS YOUR LAST CHANCE, SCUMBAG.
> CONFESS OR ELSE!

This was the email that greeted me at work on Tuesday morning. I was reaching my breaking point. Last night, I had managed to get my first good night's sleep in days, but now my nightmare was starting all over again.

My fingers banging against the keyboard, I typed:

> FUCKING JERK! IF YOU HAVE SOMETHING
> TO SAY, SAY IT TO MY FUCKING FACE!

Then I added:

> COWARD!!!!!

I clicked SEND.

The rest of the morning was pleasantly uneventful. A number of people from the office, including Bob, were attending an off-site seminar, so the atmosphere was more laid-back than usual. I worked the phones most of the morning, checking in at several project sites, and I made a few sales calls. For a while, I actually managed to lose myself in my work.

Then, late in the morning, a woman called me asking to speak with Richard Segal. The voice wasn't at all familiar and I had a feeling that the call wasn't business-related.

"This is he," I said cautiously.

"I don't know if you remember me," the woman said, "but my name's Kirsten Gale. We met in Stockbridge a few weeks ago."

I remembered Kirsten right away, looking so perfect in that white tennis dress, making orgasmic squeals every time her racket made contact with the ball, but I had absolutely no idea why she could be calling me.

"Sorry to bother you at work," she went on, "but I didn't know how else to get in touch with you. There were a bunch of Richard Segals listed, but I remembered how you said you worked for some consulting company. At first I thought it was Middletown Consulting, but there was nothing listed for that, then it hit me – you said it was Midtown Consulting. Anyway, I'm glad I got in touch with you."

Her rambling reminded me of how vacuous she had seemed in Stockbridge.

"So what's this all about?" I asked.

"Well," she said, "it has to do with your wife... Paula."

"What about Paula?" I was still confused, but a picture was starting to come into focus.

"Not just about your wife. About your wife and my fiancé. My *ex*-fiancé."

"They're having an affair," I said matter-of-factly.

There was a long pause, then Kirsten said, "How did you know?"

"I didn't know," I said, suddenly dazed and light-headed. I felt like I had just found out that someone had died. "So it's true. They *are* having an affair?"

"I don't get it," Kirsten said. "So you already know about them then?"

180

"No, I didn't know about anything until now." My face was burning up. I was starting to shake. "How did you find this out?"

"I still don't get it," Kirsten said.

"Are they having an affair or aren't they, goddamn it?!"

"Why are you yelling at me? I was just calling you to tell you that my ex-fiancé is in love with your wife. But if you already know –"

"How did you find out about this?"

"Doug broke up with me last week. He said it was because he'd met someone else. At first he wouldn't tell me who – then he said it was your wife. Can you believe that fucking asshole? I mean I could understand if he just wanted to break up – but to break up with me to be with a married woman? My friends told me it was a blessing in disguise, that he was a loser anyway and I'll be better off without him. I know this must be bad news for you, but I just thought you'd want to know. I know if I were you I'd want to know."

I thanked Kirsten for the call and then I went outside to get some air. I bumped into a couple of people on the sidewalk, including a young Latino guy who wanted to fight me. He was saying, "Come back here, bitch, and we'll go right now. Come back here," but I kept walking.

I felt like the world's biggest sucker. All this time I thought Paula and I had "repaired" our relationship and we were becoming so close, she had been screwing some arrogant stockbroker.

I recalled how Doug worked on Wall Street, probably not far from Paula. I imagined them checking into some downtown hotel under a phony name during their lunch hour or on the nights Paula had to "work late." For all I knew Doug wasn't Paula's only lover. Maybe she was just as big a slut now as she had been in junior high school. Maybe she was fucking everybody in her office, which would explain how she had gotten that promotion.

I continued downtown, past the Port Authority Bus Terminal, then I turned around and headed back toward my office.

I passed Bob in the hallway.

"Were you at a meeting?" he asked.

"Yeah," I said without stopping.

"I didn't see it on your schedule."

"I forgot to put it there," I said.

I realized that I had been curt with Bob, that I would have to apologize later, but right now I had more important things on my mind.

I called Paula. I was expecting her assistant to answer and say that Paula was at lunch – i.e., sucking Doug's dick – but Paula picked up herself.

"Hi, honey," I said sweetly.

"Oh, hi, hon," she said. "I'm on the other line. Can I call you right back?"

She was probably on the phone with Doug.

"That's all right, sweetheart," I said. "I just called to see when you'll be home tonight."

"About seven-thirty, eight o'clock. I have to stay late tonight."

"Of course you do."

"What's wrong?" she asked.

"Nothing's wrong," I said. "What makes you think something's wrong?"

"You sound strange."

"Strange? Why do I sound strange?"

"Look, I have to take this other call. I'll call you right back."

"That's okay, I'm going to be busy most of the day too. I'll just see you at home, sweetie."

"I wish you'd tell me what's wrong."

"Nothing's wrong. Have a wonderful day."

After I hung up, I whispered, "Slut."

Concentrating on work was impossible. My phone rang

182

several times during the afternoon, but I let my voicemail pick up and then I listened to the messages. There was one message from Paula, but I decided not to call her back.

I was getting stir crazy so I left work early, at around four-thirty. Like yesterday, I covered with a bogus appointment on my calendar. As I headed home I was getting more and more upset. Fearing I might say or do something I'd regret, I stopped at the Subway Inn, a dive bar on East Sixtieth Street near Lexington Avenue. I knew that having a drink or two might not be the best idea in the world, but alcohol always took the edge off, and I figured anything was better than going home sober.

I ordered a Scotch and soda. I put the glass up to my lips and paused, asking myself, "Do you really want to do this?" Myself said, "You bet." I swallowed the drink in one steady stream. Suddenly, my problems with Paula didn't seem so bad. So she was fucking a stockbroker. It was going to be a difficult time, of course, but one way or another we'd get through it. It definitely wasn't going to be the end of the world.

I guess I should have left the bar after that first drink. Ordering my fourth and fifth drinks were probably mistakes too. But it was too late for regrets – the alcohol was already in my bloodstream. When I stood up from the barstool I almost fell down. I stumbled out into the muggy twilight. The bar was near Bloomingdale's so there were plenty of people around. The sidewalk felt like it was moving as I walked toward Third Avenue, close to the building on my left, to avoid bumping into people. All the optimism I'd had while I was getting drunk was gone. Now I was just bitter and hurt. I decided this was because I was losing my buzz, so I stopped at a liquor store and bought a small bottle of Kahlúa. Like a Bowery bum, I drank straight from the bottle, which was wrapped in a paper bag. It was too late when I realized that mixing Scotch and Kahlúa was a lethal combination.

I didn't know exactly where I was going. I thought I was heading home and I somehow wound up on York Avenue, several blocks out of the way. I concentrated on the street signs and gradually made my way to East Sixty-fourth Street. By the time I reached my building I was completely trashed.

I steadied myself before I passed my doorman. Trying to act sober, I focused on maintaining my balance, but I sensed I wasn't fooling him.

I tossed my suit jacket onto the floor in the foyer and then I went to pee. Standing over the bowl I felt dizzy and my urine sprayed wildly onto the floor and all over my pants legs. Without bothering to clean up, I went to the living room and sat on the couch, continuing to drink Kahlúa. The room was spinning and there were at least two Otises asleep on the ottoman across from me. I had almost finished the bottle when Paula arrived.

"Hi, how are you?" she said. She must not have noticed that her supposedly recovering alcoholic husband was slumped drunk on the couch, clutching a bottle of Kahlúa, because she went into the bedroom without another word. It seemed like several seconds later she returned, although it must have been several minutes later because she was wearing shorts and a long T-shirt.

"I had a really shitty day and I'm starving," she said. "You in the mood for Chinese or Vietnamese?" Then she must've taken a good look at me for the first time because she said, "Oh my God! What's going on? Have you been *drinking*?"

"You noticed," I slurred. "It took you fucking long enough."

"I can't believe this. What's the matter with you?"

"You tell me," I said.

"Tell you? Tell you what?"

"Tell me," I said. "Just tell me."

"You're drunk and you're not making any sense. Did

something happen with the police today? Did they come back to your office? Is that why –"

"Just tell me, damn it," I said.

"Fine, you don't want to talk about it, don't talk about it."

She headed toward the kitchen. I went after her, accidentally knocking a vase off the coffee table. It smashed on the floor and Otis started barking.

"Look what you did!" Paula yelled over the screeching dog. "What the hell is wrong with you?"

"Tell me," I said. "Just fucking tell me."

"Tell you what?"

"You know what. Don't tell me you don't know what. You know what the fuck I'm talking about, bitch."

"Why are you doing this?" she said, starting to cry. "What's wrong with you?"

I grabbed her shoulders and started shaking her. Otis was still barking.

"Tell me," I said. "Tell me, damn it!"

"Let go of me!"

"Tell me! Tell me!"

Paula was crying hysterically. I realized that I was starting to lose control and that was exactly what I didn't want to happen. Just because she had hurt me didn't mean I had to hurt her back. I was better than her – I didn't have to stoop to her level.

I loosened my grip on her shoulders and said in a calmer voice, "Tell me. Just be honest and tell me and I'll forgive you. I promise."

Still crying, Paula said, "Why?… Why are you doing this again? Why?"

Otis was barking louder – shrieking. I yelled, "Shut the fuck up!" and the dog ran away. Then I said to Paula, "Tell me about you and Doug. Just tell me, for Christ's sake!"

Suddenly, Paula stopped crying and her blue eyes widened.

"Is that what you think?" she said. "Well, you're wrong. There's nothing going on with us. There never was."

"You're lying."

"I'm not lying. I'm telling you the truth."

"You're always lying to me! All you do is fucking lie! Even when you say you're on my side, you're still lying!"

"I'm *not* lying," she said with tears dripping down her cheeks.

"Kirsten called me," I said. "You remember Kirsten, don't you?... Don't you?!"

"What did she tell you?"

"I see you're not denying it anymore."

"Look, I really don't care what you think happened, all right? I just want you to know I'm not going to forgive you for this – ever!"

Paula marched by me and Otis joined her in the bedroom, just beating the fast-closing door. I remained near the kitchen, swaying drunkenly.

I didn't feel like being home with Paula, even with her in the other room, so I took the bottle of Kahlúa and left the apartment.

I stumbled around the neighborhood until I'd finished the bottle, then I wandered into a bar on First Avenue. It was crowded with kids in their twenties, but I managed to get a seat at the bar. Screaming over the pulsing music, I ordered a Scotch and soda. I don't remember drinking it but my glass somehow wound up empty. I ordered another and took a sip, when a guy bumped into me. Next thing I knew, we were standing up, facing each other, and I was saying "Fuck you" and "I'll kick your ass." He was bigger than me, and younger, but that didn't stop me. I took a swing at him, or at least I *tried* to. He grabbed my limp arm and started laughing. I spat in his face, then he let go of my arm and started punching me. I fell onto the floor and he was kicking the shit out of me, but it didn't hurt as much as I knew it should. Then the bouncer, a big Italian-looking guy, came over and picked me up. He pushed me outside and I must have tried to go after him, too, or said something to him, because he had me against a brick wall, and started punching me in the face. People were standing around, cheering and laughing. Later, I was lying on the sidewalk in a fetal position, tasting blood on my lips, wondering how I was going to explain all this to the guys at A.A.

18

When I opened my eyes I couldn't breathe through my nose. I took a deep breath, inhaling whatever was clogging my nostrils, then I noticed a disgusting odor. It smelled like a combination of rotting milk and urine. I thought I must still be outside, in the garbage, then I gradually realized that I was home in bed and that the disgusting odor was coming from me.

My whole body hurt. I was too dizzy and nauseous to move. My throat was sore and dry and my breath smelled like vomit. I closed my eyes, wanting to fall back asleep, then I realized that the light shining against my eyelids was daylight coming through the venetian blinds. I opened my eyes again and turned painfully in the direction of the digital clock on the night table. The digits read 10:23. I was convinced that I was dreaming or reading the clock wrong – it couldn't be so late. Maybe it was 5:23 or 6:23 – that was more like it. But after several seconds I realized that the time I was seeing was correct – it was ten twenty-three and I had to attend a sales meeting at eleven o'clock.

I stood out of bed too suddenly and my knees buckled and I fell down. I coughed up the taste of Kahlúa and Scotch. I stood up and stumbled into the bathroom, cringing from the pain in my legs and stomach. I was bare-chested, but I was still wearing the pants and dress shoes I had worn to work yesterday. After I peed, I looked in the mirror, shocked by the sight. One of my eyes was purple and swollen, and crusted blood or vomit surrounded my mouth. There were also deep scratches on my cheek that had been bleeding and were starting to scab. I figured a cat must have scratched me while I was lying in the garbage. I took off my damp pants and went into the shower and scrubbed myself clean as quickly and as efficiently as I could. When I came out, I still felt and looked horrible, but I couldn't afford to take the day off. I had a ton of work to do and missing a sales meeting would be a bad move if I wanted to stay on track for a promotion.

I was angry at myself for getting so drunk and I swore that I would never drink again. Then I remembered about the fight I'd had with Paula before I went out last night.

"Paula!"

There was no answer. What was I thinking? She must have left for work three hours ago.

I opened the bedroom door and Otis started barking at me. Vaguely, I remembered how I'd yelled at him last night when I came home from drinking.

"All right, take it easy," I said. The barking was aggravating my hangover. "Just shut the hell up!"

But Otis continued to bark, growling and jumping against my legs, as I went into the living room.

When I'd gotten home last night, stumbling drunk, Paula had been in bed next to me. But I must have disgusted her so much that she had gone to sleep on the couch.

Or maybe she had spent the night at Doug's.

I dressed for work, then I took Otis out for his walk. The dog still didn't seem like his usual self, probably still holding a grudge for last night.

The eleven o'clock sales meeting was already in progress when I entered the conference room through a back door and took a seat at the long table. There were seven or eight people in the room, including Bob, who was standing by the dry-erase board, and everyone looked at me when I walked in, with a combined expression of fascination and disgust.

Bob tried to continue with the meeting, as if nothing were wrong, but I was too much of a distraction so he finally said, "Are you all right, Richard?"

"Fine," I said, knowing this answer was ridiculous considering how I looked.

"What *happened*?"

"I'll tell you all about it later," I said. "It was no big deal – really."

Bob went on, talking about a minor change in the company's commission structure.

When the meeting ended and everyone left the room except Bob and me, Bob said, "So, what the hell happened to you?"

"It was the craziest thing," I said, smiling. "My wife and I were walking by a construction site last night and one of the construction workers shouted something. Paula gave the guy the finger and the guy said something back. Next thing I knew I was fighting this construction worker. Well, not exactly fighting him, as you can see."

Bob was staring at me. I had a feeling that he didn't believe my story, but that he didn't want to go to the effort of figuring out why I was lying either.

"Well, I'm sorry that happened," he said. "Are you going to press charges?"

"Charges?"

"Against the construction worker."

"No. I mean maybe. I don't know, to tell you the truth I'm just a little embarrassed about the whole situation."

"If you want to take the rest of the day off you can," he said. "You could probably use the rest."

"That's all right," I said. "I have a lot to do today and I want to get to it. Don't worry, I'm all right. I mean this won't get in the way of anything."

Despite two cups of black coffee, I could barely stay awake at my desk. The caffeine only seemed to intensify the throbbing in my face. I'd already checked my email log once and I checked it again, relieved to see that I had received no new threats.

I made a few phone calls, but I knew it was going to

be impossible to get any work done. This was extremely frustrating because I wanted nothing more than to get my career back in full gear, but I couldn't, and I knew it was all my fault for getting drunk. I was going to have to keep going to A.A. meetings and finally admit to myself that I had a serious problem.

When I woke up someone was tapping me on the shoulder. I didn't know where I was, then I recognized Bob's face.

"Go home, Richard – get some rest."

"I'm sorry," I said, still disoriented. "I didn't mean –"

"We'll discuss it some other time," Bob said. "Just go."

There were two messages on my home answering machine from Paula's office. The first was from Sheila, Paula's assistant, asking if Paula was planning to come into work today. The second call was from Chris, Paula's boss. In a serious, concerned tone, Chris said that he had "missed" Paula at a meeting this morning, and asked her to please call him as soon as she got this message.

It was very odd for Paula not to show up at work without calling. She had probably spent the day with Doug. I imagined them together – their naked, sweaty bodies in bed – but I tried not to let it get to me.

Otis was still acting unusually upset – barking and growling. I decided that he was probably angry about all the tension in the apartment lately. I petted his head, which calmed him for a while, but then he started acting up again.

While I wanted Paula back more than anything, I also realized that the situation was out of my control. If she didn't love me anymore and she wanted to be with another man there was nothing I could do. But if she still loved me and wanted to keep working on our problems I was willing to do that, too. It was all up to her.

I undressed and got into bed, passing out quickly. When I woke up I was still exhausted, but at least my hangover symptoms were gone. It was after five o'clock. I still felt awful for having to leave work early. I'd probably made a fool of myself and I knew I'd definitely have to apologize to Bob tomorrow.

Otis was still making a racket.

"Come on, dog, get over it, for Christ's sake," I said.

But Otis barked again, louder. I'd had enough. I put him in my office and shut the door. He was still barking, but the noise was mostly muffled.

I ordered Chinese food for dinner and ate out of the foil containers in front of the TV. I fell asleep on the couch and was awakened by a phone call.

"Is Paula there?"

"Who's calling?" I asked drowsily.

There was a long pause, then the man said, "This is Doug Pearson – remember, we played tennis in Stockbridge."

Still half-asleep, it took me a few moments to put it all together – Doug, the guy who had probably been fucking my wife nonstop for the past twenty-four hours, was now calling me.

"What the hell do you want?"

Suddenly, I was wide awake.

"Is Paula there or not?" he asked.

Who the hell did this guy think he was, calling my apartment?

"You've got some fucking nerve," I said.

"I want to speak with Paula."

"She's not here."

"Where is she?"

"You'd know that better than I would."

"I want to speak to her."

"I said she's not here. And if you ever call here again –"

"You better not've hurt her again," he said. "If you did, I swear to God I'll kill you."

"Hurt her?" I said. "What the hell are you talking about?"

"You're never gonna get her back," he went on. "It's over with you two so you might as well admit it."

"We'll see about that," I said.

Doug hung up. I slammed the portable phone down onto the coffee table so hard the battery pack popped out. I was about to lose it completely. I couldn't believe Doug had the balls to call my apartment.

Then, settling down, I started worrying about Paula again. If she wasn't with Doug and she didn't go in to work today, then where the hell was she? She could have slept at a hotel last night, but wouldn't she have called me, or her boss, or *someone* by now?

I remembered the email: CONFESS, OR ELSE! Maybe the person who'd been sending the messages had kidnapped or hurt Paula because I hadn't confessed to killing Michael Rudnick. The idea seemed crazy, but it also seemed like there had to be some connection. Paula disappearing right after I'd received the threats was just too coincidental.

I went into the kitchen and drank lukewarm water straight from the faucet. On my way back to the living room, I passed through the dining room, and stopped still when I spotted Paula's pocketbook on a chair adjacent to the dining room table. Although sometimes she went short distances without her pocketbook – to the supermarket or to do an errand in the neighborhood – she never went to work without it.

Now I was even more convinced that something horrible had happened. Paula didn't have any close friends in the city – not anyone I could imagine her going to stay with. I supposed she could have had a lover I didn't know about, but I couldn't see her going anywhere for so long without her pocketbook.

I wondered if I should start calling hospitals, or even the police. Then I decided to calm down – there had to be some simple explanation for all of this. Maybe Paula had taken a day off work to be by herself. She may have called her office, but there was some mix-up and her colleagues didn't get the message. She could show up at the apartment at any moment.

I paced in the foyer and the hallway for about half an hour, steadily losing hope that Paula was okay. By nine o'clock, I was seriously considering calling the police. The last thing I needed was more police in my life, but I knew that time could be valuable and if I waited any longer I might be putting Paula in danger.

I started dialing 911, but on the second 1 I hung up. It seemed crazy to call the police when I was still a murder suspect. I figured that the New Jersey police had probably contacted the New York police about me and I definitely didn't want to complicate things. Besides, even if the New York police had no idea that I had been questioned about Rudnick's murder, I wouldn't be able to tell them about the threatening emails I'd been receiving, which would probably be their best lead for finding Paula.

I decided to give it another day. For all I knew I would wake up and Paula would be in bed next to me.

In the locked room, Otis was still making a racket. I went to check on him and see if I could get him to calm down, when I saw that he had shat and pissed all over the floor.

"Goddamn it, dog!" I yelled. "What the hell is wrong with you?!"

Otis ran out of the room and I chased him around the apartment. Finally, I caught him in the living room and I picked him up and spanked him. Then I dropped him on the floor and he scampered away into the kitchen.

19

"I'm glad you came in here on your own to talk to me this morning," Bob said, "because, to tell you the truth, I did a lot of thinking last night, and if you didn't start showing me this kind of responsibility for your actions I was probably going to let you go today."

I was sitting across from Bob in his office. I hadn't slept well and I was struggling to stay awake.

"Thank you so much," I said. "Believe me, I only have one goal, and that's to make a lot of money – for myself and for the company. From now on, I'm going to be completely dedicated – I'll even start working nights and weekends if I have to."

"All right, let's not get carried away," Bob said. "This is just a job – I want you to have a life too. All I ask from my employees is that, while they're in this office, they give me one-hundred-percent dedication. You think you can do that from now on?"

My cellphone rang and I answered it, hoping it was Paula. Instead the call was from Jim Turner at Loomis & Caldwell. I instantly remembered how I'd made an appointment to meet Jim at his office at nine o'clock this morning to discuss his hardware quotes. It was close to ten now.

"Oh my God, I'm so sorry," I said. "I'll leave right now. I can be there in ten minutes, I promise."

Jim said he was tied up for the rest of the day and he sounded bitter and annoyed. When I suggested meeting tomorrow he said he had a call coming in on another line and he hung up on me.

"Who was that?" Bob asked accusingly.

He had heard too much of the conversation, so there was no way I could cover with a lie. I explained the situation, then Bob said:

"We can't lose this sale, Richard. That's an eighty-thousand-dollar client – maybe more – and he hasn't paid us anything yet."

"We won't lose him," I said.

"It sounds like you may've lost him already."

"I don't know how this happened," I said. "I guess I just left here so suddenly yesterday that I forgot to print out a copy of my next day's appointments, the way I usually do, and –"

"This can't go on any longer," Bob said. "I'm trying to run a business here and every day there's a new crisis with you."

"I'll reschedule the meeting," I said.

"You'd better," Bob said. "If you can't, that's it. No more second chances."

I spent the rest of the morning trying to get hold of Jim Turner. His secretary kept giving me the runaround, insisting that he couldn't come to the phone. Finally, around noon, I was able to get through.

He sounded even more upset than he had been before, saying, "Maybe I'll just have to find a company that *wants* my business," and I knew I had to resort to desperate measures. Completely humiliating myself, I started crying, telling him that my job was on the line.

"Please give us another chance," I begged. "If I lose this sale my whole life'll be ruined. Please."

The strategy worked. Turner said that he would be out of the office most of the day tomorrow, but that he would be in my neighborhood in the afternoon, and we agreed to meet at one o'clock at my office to discuss the quotes. I thanked him again and again, telling him what a great guy he was and how much I appreciated him helping me out this way.

When I hung up, my shirt was drenched in sweat and I let out a deep breath. Then I remembered that Paula was still missing and I picked up the phone again.

I had called Paula's office early in the morning, before nine, and left a message on her tape, apologizing for being such a jerk the other night, and to please call me as soon as she got this message. Now I called again and Paula's assistant transferred me to Chris, who had left the message on my tape last night. Chris asked me if I had heard anything and when I said no he asked me if I'd called the police. Thinking fast, I said, "Yes, first thing this morning." Chris asked me if I had any idea where Paula could be and I said "no", I was completely baffled. He asked me to call him as soon as I heard anything and I gave him my office phone number and asked him to do the same.

Now I knew I couldn't put it off any longer. I had to call the police right away.

An operator transferred me to my local precinct. I waited on hold for a while and then a Detective John Himoto came on the line and said that the precinct had already received a call about Paula Borowski's apparent disappearance from a man named Doug Pearson this morning. I was about to explain how I hadn't called sooner because I was hoping to hear from Paula, when Himoto interrupted and asked if I could come to the precinct or if he could stop by my apartment sometime this afternoon. Realizing that there was no way I could leave early and still have a job, I said, "Okay, how's five-thirty?"

"So tell me more about this fight you had with this construction worker?" Detective Himoto asked, sitting across from me at the dining room table. Himoto had a large, round face and a receding hairline. He looked native Japanese, but he spoke English with a hardened Bronx accent.

Although I hadn't felt comfortable lying to Himoto about who had beaten me up, I'd had to stick to the construction-worker story just in case Himoto, for some reason, decided to speak with Bob. I already sensed that Himoto didn't trust me. I figured this was probably because Doug had told him that I had pushed Paula into the wall that time, so Himoto figured that if something bad had happened to Paula then I probably had something to do with it. I didn't know if he had already spoken with the New Jersey police, or with someone else from the New York police, and found out that I was a suspect in the Michael Rudnick murder case. Obviously, I wasn't planning to bring the subject up myself.

"It was just like I told you," I said. "Paula and I were taking a walk, a construction worker said something, and one thing led to another. But I don't see why this has anything to do with –"

"Which construction site was this?" Himoto asked.

"Excuse me?" Suddenly, my face was burning, like I had a fever.

"Where did this altercation take place?"

Jesus, I thought, why didn't I just tell him the truth? Now I was just digging myself deeper and deeper into a hole.

I tried to remember the sites where construction was taking place in the neighborhood. There was a building going up on Lexington... or was it Third?

"I think it was Third Avenue," I said. "I really don't remember."

"Third and what?"

"Somewhere in the Sixties."

"Can't you be any more specific?"

"Sorry. Can't we just concentrate on my wife?"

"That's what I'm trying to do, Mr Segal. I know this is hard for you, but if you could just bear with me." He turned a page on his notepad. "So you and your wife take a walk at around eight o'clock, and this is when a construction worker beats you up."

"That's right," I said.

"I thought construction workers break at five."

"I don't really know if he was a construction worker," I said. "He could have just been a guy hanging out near a construction site."

"Got it," Himoto said skeptically. "So after you take this walk you return to your apartment at around eight-thirty. When was the last time you saw your wife?"

"It must have been about eleven o'clock," I said.

"That late?" Himoto asked.

"I went out," I said. "I had a couple of drinks. When I came home Paula was in bed."

"Did you have a couple of drinks or were you drunk?"

If Himoto had spoken to my doorman he already knew I was drunk. I decided that there was no point in making up any more stories.

"Let's put it this way – I had a couple of drinks too many," I said.

"Doug Pearson said you were drunk that night. He said you came home from work drunk and then you had an argument with your wife."

"How the hell would Doug Pearson know what happened?"

"He said your wife called him at approximately nine P.M. What I'm wondering about is if you came home from work drunk, when did you and your wife take this walk you said you took? Were you drunk when you took the walk?"

"Doug is lying."

"Lying about what?"

"Everything. I'm telling you the way it happened. I had a drink or two after work, but I wasn't drunk. I came home, took a walk with Paula, then I went out drinking alone."

"And you didn't have a fight with your wife?"

"It wasn't a fight, it was an *argument* – a minor argument. You know, if I were you I wouldn't pay much attention to anything Doug Pearson says. He was having an affair with my wife and he just wants to make me look as bad as possible."

"What makes you say Doug Pearson was having an affair with your wife?" Himoto asked. There was a strange tone in his voice – I didn't know if he was suspicious or just curious.

"His fiancée... I mean, his *ex*-fiancée called me up at work and told me."

"According to what Mr Pearson told me, he hadn't been having an affair with your wife at all."

"He's lying," I said. "He has something to do with this and he's trying to cover for himself."

Himoto seemed unconvinced and I couldn't help wondering myself if maybe I'd been wrong about Paula and Doug – maybe they weren't having an affair after all. It had been stupid of me to take Kirsten's word for it.

Himoto turned to a new page on his notepad and said, "Mr Pearson also told me that the first time your wife came to his apartment was about two weeks ago, after you pushed her into a wall – I guess that was during one of your 'minor arguments'. Then, on this past Tuesday night, Mr Pearson says your wife called him again, apparently afraid you were going to become violent, and Mr Pearson told her to come to his apartment right away. She declined the offer and said that she was going to go out to take a walk and get some fresh air."

"I don't believe this," I said. "You actually think... I told you, my wife was home when I came home from drinking."

"I'm just telling you what Mr Pearson told me. Chris Dolan, your wife's boss, also called the precinct today, and he also raised some concern about you. He said your wife came to work a couple of weeks ago with a bruise on her cheek –"

"She fell in the shower."

"That's what Mr Dolan said your wife claimed happened,

but there were fears in her office that domestic violence might have been involved."

"Come on, I would never hurt my wife," I said. "Are you out of your fucking mind?"

"Excuse me?"

"Accusing me of something like that. You have to be crazy to –"

"All right, let's calm down," Himoto said.

"No, you calm down," I said. "My wife is missing and your job is to find her, so just find her, damn it!"

Himoto shifted on the couch.

"I'm just trying to get a sense of your wife's whereabouts on Tuesday night," he said, "what she might've been thinking about, what her emotional state was, and then I'm going to try to piece all of this information together and reach a logical conclusion. This is the way I run my investigations – I'm sorry if you have a problem with that."

"Just find her," I said. "That's all I care about. Find her."

Himoto was looking into my eyes again. I became uncomfortable and I had to look away.

"So you're telling me that the last time you saw your wife was on Tuesday evening in bed at approximately eleven P.M."

"That's correct," I said. "When I got into bed she was there next to me."

"Are any of your wife's belongings missing?"

"No," I said. "At least not that I'm aware of."

"Did she take any money with her, credit cards…"

"She left her pocketbook," I said.

Himoto's eyes widened.

"Does she usually leave home without her pocketbook?"

"No, not usually. But I suppose she could have just taken some money and left – if she was in a hurry."

"Do you think your wife was suicidal, Mr Segal?"

"Paula? No way."

"She never talked about wanting to kill herself – even a

time when you thought she might not be serious?"

"No, I – well, that's not really true. Actually, several days ago, she was telling me about problems she had when she was a teenager. Anyway, she said she once went into her parents' car inside a garage and turned on the ignition. But she was very depressed at that time and I don't think she would ever try something like that *now*."

"The only reason I'm suggesting this," Himoto said, "is you're telling me you had an argument the other night, and according to Doug Pearson the idea of divorce was mentioned. Perhaps it's not such a leap to imagine her becoming overly distressed about the situation."

I tried to imagine the scene – Paula leaving the apartment and taking a cab to the Brooklyn Bridge. I saw her standing on the bridge's railing, looking down at the pitch-black East River with a crazed expression.

"Maybe it's something to look into," I said, "but I don't think so – not Paula."

"What about enemies?" Himoto asked. "Was there anyone who was angry at her for any reason?"

"No," I said. "Nobody."

"What about you?" Himoto asked.

"What about me?" I asked, wondering if he was accusing me again.

"Do you have any enemies?"

Thinking about the emails, I said, "No. No one."

Himoto closed his notepad.

"Let us know if anyone tries to contact you," he said, "although, to be quite honest, given that approximately forty-eight hours have elapsed since your wife disappeared and you haven't heard anything, it doesn't seem likely that kidnapping for ransom could have been the motive. But you never know."

"So what's the next move?" I asked.

"Ideally?" Himoto said. "Ideally your wife walks through the door and you two live happily ever after.

In the meantime, we'll do whatever we can to locate her, which reminds me – do you have a recent photograph of your wife?"

I went into the bedroom and returned with a picture of Paula that I had taken during our weekend in Stockbridge. I remembered how Paula had given the Jersey police a picture of me from the same packet of photos.

As Himoto put the photo away in the inside pocket of his sport jacket I said, "I wish you wouldn't pay attention to anything Doug Pearson says about me. I don't know if he was having an affair with my wife or not, but I do know that he *wanted* to be with her. He called here last night, asking if I knew where Paula was and, if you want my opinion, he sounded obsessed. He told me 'You're never gonna get her back' and 'It's over between you two.' I don't want to accuse the guy of anything – I mean, I hardly even know him – but maybe you should be asking *him* where my wife is."

For the first time, I had the sense that Himoto was on my side.

"Is the doorman who's on duty now the same doorman who was on duty Tuesday night?" Himoto asked.

"Yes," I said.

"Maybe we should go down and ask him a few questions."

I went down with Himoto to talk to Raymond. Raymond said that someone had come to visit Paula the night she disappeared.

"He was in a suit," Raymond said. "He had dark hair."

"That must have been Doug," I said.

But Raymond said he couldn't remember what time the man arrived at the building, how long he had stayed, or if he had left alone or with Paula.

"I only take a good look at the people who are coming into the building," Raymond said, "not at the people who are going out."

Himoto asked Raymond some more questions, but Raymond could offer no further help. Raymond suggested that Himoto might want to call the building's security company to view the footage from the lobby's camera. After Himoto took down the name and phone number of the security company, I said, "See, I told you Doug has something to do with this."

"But you said your wife was home when you came home from drinking."

"She *was* home," I said, "but Doug was here that night and he didn't tell you that when you talked to him, right? That could mean he's trying to hide something, right?"

"It definitely raises some suspicion," Himoto said.

"So are you gonna talk to him again? Find out if he knows anything?"

"Don't worry, we'll follow up every lead we have ASAP," Himoto said. "I'll let you know if there's any news, and if you hear anything I hope you'll do the same."

After Himoto left, I remained in the lobby for a while, talking to Raymond about Paula.

"I'm sure she's okay," Raymond said. "She'll probably come home tonight. You'll see."

"I hope you're right," I said. My eyes were starting to tear. "If something happened to her, I don't know what I'd do."

"She'll be okay," he said. "Don't worry."

Back in my apartment, I broke down crying. All the stress of the past few days had built up and become unbearable. I kneeled on the floor in the foyer, sobbing uncontrollably.

Later, as I started to recover, I was thinking about Doug, wondering if he was really capable of hurting Paula. I remembered how intense he had been on the tennis court, grunting like a madman every time his racket made contact with the ball. It wasn't such a stretch to imagine him as a psychopathic murderer.

Pacing the apartment, I imagined what had happened

on Tuesday night. Paula had called Doug around nine o'clock. She was very upset, so Doug had insisted on coming over to see her, whether she wanted to see him or not. Doug stayed for a while, trying to get Paula to come home with him. Feeling guilty for having an affair, Paula turned Doug down and Doug left alone around ten o'clock. Then when I came home, around eleven – drunk, smelly, and beaten up – Paula was so repulsed that she decided to go to Doug's place after all. Then something happened. Maybe Paula and Doug had some kind of fight. Paula decided to break it off with him and Doug became jealous and enraged. I saw Doug, his face red and intense, beating up Paula, then killing her.

I was clenching my fists so tightly my fingernails were cutting into my palms. I wanted to find out where Doug lived and go confront him, but I knew this was exactly what he wanted me to do. He'd already told lies about me to Himoto, and he'd probably been sending the emails to me too. Paula had probably told him that the police had questioned me about a murder, so he came up with the brilliant idea of harassing me.

Then I thought of *something* I could do.

I went into my office in the spare bedroom and tossed Otis out into the hallway. I still hadn't cleaned up his piss and shit from the floor and the entire room stank.

I booted up my computer, then dialed into my PC at work and accessed my email account. I retrieved one of the threatening messages and replied:

FUCK YOU DOUG.

I clicked SEND then turned off the computer. After I cleaned up Otis's mess, I took a long, cold shower.

Throughout the evening, I checked my work email several times, but I had no new messages. Around midnight, I took Otis down for his walk. He was better behaved than he had been recently, but he seemed a little sad.

"I know," I said. "I miss Mommy too."

The apartment seemed noticeably empty and quiet without Paula. To create some noise, I turned on the TV in the bedroom, but this only made the atmosphere more depressing. I wondered if this was a preview of the rest of my life, if I'd always be alone, in an empty apartment, with a TV going in the background.

I cried again for a while, letting the tears run freely down my face, then I flicked off the TV and got into bed. Usually, the noise of Third Avenue traffic was a constant in my apartment, but tonight the city seemed unusually silent.

When I woke up I went right to my computer and checked my email, but there was still no response to my message.

Himoto hadn't called so I decided to call the precinct to find out if there was any news. A woman who answered said that, as far as she knew, there hadn't been any developments, but that she would leave a message with Himoto that I had called.

It was raining steadily when I left for work but, miraculously, I was able to hail a cab on the corner of Lexington and Sixty-fourth. I realized that it probably wasn't helping my cause to go in to work today. Most men whose wives are missing would stay home, awaiting any word from the police. I would have stayed home, but I couldn't miss my meeting with Jim Turner.

At my cubicle, I logged onto my computer right away and checked my email, but there was still no response. I called Himoto and managed to speak with him briefly. He said he had spoken to Doug and Doug had admitted that he had come to visit Paula on Tuesday evening at around nine-thirty, but he claimed he had stayed at the apartment only for about ten minutes.

"Why didn't he tell you this before?" I asked.

"He said he didn't think it was important," Himoto said.

"Give me a break," I said. "It's obvious he's hiding something."

Himoto said he was going to follow up on some more leads and that he would be in touch by the end of the day.

I confirmed the one o'clock meeting with Jim Turner by leaving a message with his secretary. At ten o'clock, I attended an internal sales meeting, to discuss the status of our current projects and to make sure we had the right personnel in place. I spoke about my projects with Jim Turner and Don Chaney. The whole time, I was distracted, worrying about Paula, and my presentation was disjointed and rambling. As I was talking, I couldn't help noticing how Steve Ferguson was smirking, whispering something to John Hennessy. When I was through speaking I glared at Steve and he looked back at me defiantly. Our standoff lasted for several seconds, then I looked away.

When the meeting ended, I returned to my cubicle and checked my email log.

WHO THE HELL IS DOUG?

I'M SICK OF YOUR BULLSHIT.

TWELVE NOON AT TEXAS ARIZONA

ON RIVER STREET IN HOBOKEN.

NO MORE GAMES.

20

I took the D train from Forty-seventh Street and switched for the PATH train at Thirty-fourth. At a little before twelve, I arrived at Texas Arizona, a casual restaurant directly across the street from the Hoboken train station.

When I entered the bar area a waitress came over to me by the door and asked me how many.

"Two," I said. "I think."

"You think?"

"A table for two would be fine," I said.

There were only about ten other customers in the whole place. I looked around, but I didn't recognize anyone and no one seemed to recognize me.

The waitress led me to a table by the window and I sat down facing the entrance. She asked me if she could get me a drink while I was waiting. I asked for an iced tea.

Some Springsteen song was playing on the restaurant's stereo. I stared out the window, sipping the iced tea, watching the street in front of the bar and the entrance to the train station. I figured that Doug had sent me the latest email, pretending not to be himself. I imagined him crossing the street and then sitting across from me, confessing that he had murdered Paula. Then I imagined myself leaping across the table and sticking a fork into his face.

I patted my forehead with a napkin.

At a quarter past twelve, I was starting to wonder if I was going to be stood up. I decided to give it another ten minutes.

I looked over and saw a big muscle-head guy in a tank top and jeans, standing near the door with his arms crossed in front of his chest. He looked like a bouncer, but I hadn't noticed him before.

Then a teenager, about sixteen years old, entered the restaurant and I nearly choked on the sip of iced tea I had just taken. I had to be asleep, having a nightmare, or maybe I was hallucinating.

The teenager stopped a few feet in front of my table and stared right at me. Now I was convinced that I was flipping out, having some sort of breakdown. Why else was I seeing a teenaged Michael Rudnick standing in front of me?

He must have enjoyed making me feel like I was losing my mind, because he didn't say a word. He just stood there, staring at me with a blank expression. Maybe he didn't look exactly like the Rudnick of old – his jaw was larger and his lips were thinner – but the similarity was still incredible. He was the same size as Rudnick used to be – big and flabby – and his face was covered with acne. He had the same dark, staring eyes that had once terrorized me. He was even wearing clothes that the young Rudnick might have worn – jeans and a big, baggy sweatshirt. But the most startling resemblance was the single dark eyebrow that stretched straight across his forehead like a thick, ugly caterpillar.

Finally, he sat down across from me, but he wouldn't stop staring. I thought about reaching across the table and trying to stick my hand through his body to test if he were real, but I didn't budge.

"You recognize me, huh?" he said.

It was incredible. Even his high-pitched voice sounded like the young Rudnick.

"Of course I recognize you," I said. "You look exactly like –"

"My father," he said.

At least I knew I wasn't losing my mind. I realized he'd probably been at the police station that day too.

The waitress came over and asked Rudnick Jr. if he wanted a drink.

209

"That's all right," he said, continuing to stare at me. "I don't think I'll be staying too long."

The waitress asked me if I wanted to order anything to eat and I shook my head. She went away.

"So what do you want from me?" I asked.

"You know what I want," he said.

"No," I said. "Actually, I don't."

"I want a confession."

"A confession to what?"

"Don't be a dick."

"If you don't tell me what you –"

"I know you killed my father."

"But I didn't kill him."

"You're lying."

"I didn't kill your father. I don't know how you got that idea."

I had a flashback to the parking lot, when I was crouched over Michael Rudnick's body, driving the knife into his groin.

"It was obviously you," Rudnick Jr. said. "Just confess to the cops already… or else."

"Or else what?" I said, wondering if he was hinting about Paula.

"Or else you'll find out what else," he said.

"I'm telling you," I said. "You're making a mistake."

"I know you did it," he said. "If you didn't do it, you wouldn't be here."

"I came here to find out who was harassing me."

"I know what happened at my father's office that day."

"Nothing happened at his office."

"You tried to attack him."

"That was just a misunderstanding."

"There were witnesses so stop fucking lying to me!"

The waitress and people from other tables were looking in our direction. The big guy came over to our table.

"Everything okay here?" he asked Rudnick Jr.

"Yeah," Rudnick Jr. said. "Everything's fine. Just hang out by the door, man. I'll be there in a few minutes."

The big guy glared at me for a few seconds, then he returned to his spot by the door.

"Friend of yours?" I asked.

"He's my bodyguard," Rudnick Jr. said.

"Bodyguard? Why do you —"

"Protection."

"Protection from who?"

"Who do you think? You killed my father. How do I know you won't try to kill me?"

"This is ridiculous," I said. "Didn't your father tell the police that a teenager attacked him in that parking lot? Do I look like a teenager?"

"Teenagers discovered him in the lot. He could've gotten confused."

"But the police questioned me about it twice. If they had any evidence don't you think they would have arrested me by now?"

"So what about the day you attacked him in his office?" Rudnick Jr. said. "You're gonna deny that, too?"

"It's true, I *was* in his office that day and we had an argument, but I didn't *attack* him."

"People were there. They saw you."

"Look, I don't want to talk to you about this because I know it'll upset you."

"Oh, so now you wanna protect me?"

"Yes," I said. "In a way I do."

"I know exactly what happened."

I paused, then I said, "How do you *know*?"

"What do you mean?"

"You said you know. How do you know?"

He was looking away now. I knew I'd hit on something.

"I just do."

"How? Did the detectives tell you? Did your mother tell you? If they did it would just be my word against your

211

father's. How do you know I'm not lying, making it all up?"

"That's not what we're talking about," Rudnick Jr. said, still avoiding eye contact.

"Come on, tell me," I said. "Did your father say something about me?"

"No."

"Then how do you know I'm not lying? You wouldn't've started sending me those emails, gone to all this trouble, if you weren't sure. Why are you so sure?"

"Fuck you," Rudnick Jr. said.

"That other kid and I weren't the only ones, were we?" I said. "Did your father play Ping-Pong with you? Did he say, 'You're gonna feel it?'"

"Shut up!"

"That's why you think I did it, isn't it? Because you wanted to kill him yourself."

"Shut up, you fuckin' son of a bitch!"

The bodyguard started toward our table again. Rudnick Jr., his face suddenly pink, motioned with his hand for him to stay away.

"I'm warning you," Rudnick Jr. said to me. "This is your last chance. Go to the phone and call the cops right now or you'll be sorry – very sorry."

I glanced at my watch – it was past twelve-thirty.

"Look, I have to get back to the city," I said to Rudnick Jr. "It seems to me that you should probably see a shrink. Your father hurt you when you were a child and you obviously haven't recovered from it yet. My wife has a good shrink in the city – Dr Carmadie, I forget the first name. You should look him up."

"Crazy son of a bitch," Rudnick Jr. said as he stood up. "I hope you rot in hell."

Rudnick Jr. stared at me menacingly for a few more seconds, then he and his bodyguard left the restaurant. As I paid my bill at the register, I glanced up at a clock on the wall – it was twelve thirty-six. I could still make it back to Manhattan in time for my meeting.

I jogged across the street to the train station. At the bottom of the stairs, someone grabbed my arms from behind. Suddenly, Rudnick Jr. was standing in front of me.

"You didn't think I'd let you get away that easy, did you?" he said.

While his bodyguard held me, Rudnick Jr. punched me several times in the face. Each punch hurt more than the one before and my head kept snapping back. I realized that he had something hard in his fist, or maybe he was wearing brass knuckles. It was difficult to breathe through my nose and I felt dizzy, like I might pass out.

After finishing off with a few solid punches to my stomach, Rudnick Jr. held a switchblade to my neck, the tip of the blade under my chin, and said, "That was for my father, you fuckin' asshole." He moved the blade higher, cutting into my skin.

"Come on," the bodyguard said, "let's get the fuck out of here."

"Confess," Rudnick Jr. said to me, "or else," then he and the bodyguard took off up the stairs.

For several seconds, I remained keeled over, trying to catch my breath. My face was sore and I was sucking blood off my lips. Finally, I limped toward the turnstile.

As I waited on the platform for a train I tried to clean myself up the best I could. I found a tissue in my back pocket and I wiped some blood off my lips. The tissue quickly turned red and was useless. My lips seemed to have stopped bleeding, but blood had dripped onto my shirt and suit jacket.

A midtown-bound train arrived quickly. People on the train were staring at me so I turned toward the door, ignoring them. In the door's Plexiglas window, I barely recognized my battered reflection.

At Thirty-fourth Street, I waited for a D train, but after five minutes there was no train in sight. Finally, at a few minutes to one a train pulled into the station. When I got out at Forty-seventh Street, I pushed through the crowd – people who looked at my face moved out of the way quickly – and then I exited the station and ran as fast as my aching ribs would allow me to run, across Sixth Avenue to my office building. In the elevator I checked my watch and saw it was five after one.

Karen, at the reception desk, said that Jim Turner was with Bob in the conference room. My face was very sore and it hurt to move my mouth, but when I entered the conference room I still managed to smile.

"Jim," I said. "Good to see you."

I extended my hand toward Jim, then saw there was blood on it and pulled it back. Bob and Jim looked horrified.

"Sorry for my appearance," I said, still smiling tensely. "I was just in a little accident on Forty-eighth Street."

"No kidding?" Jim said.

"Yeah, a bike messenger hit me," I said. "You know how crazy those guys are. Anyway, I fell down and got a little beat up, but the kid was in really bad shape. I stayed with him until the ambulance came – I think he'll make it. But enough about me, let's talk about your project."

I started to explain how our company would go about integrating the new PCs and servers into Turner's Linux network. I thought I was giving one of my better presentations, but after I'd been talking for only a couple of minutes Turner looked at his beeper and said, "Sorry, there's an emergency at my office. I have to go."

"Okey dokey," I said. "Did you want to leave a check with us today?"

"No, that's okay," he said. "I'll have to call you."

"You sure?" I said. "Because if we just get the payment out of the way today, tomorrow morning we can –"

"I'm sorry, I have to go."

When Turner had left the conference room Bob said to me, "You're fired."

"Fired?" I said, stunned. "Why? It wasn't my fault he got beeped."

"It's not because he got beeped."

"Oh, you mean the blood on my shirt. I can explain –"

"Let's not make this any more difficult than it already is. Just clear out your desk and we'll send you your final paycheck in the mail."

"Look, I know I've been acting strange lately, but I have a very good explanation."

"I don't want to hear it."

"You don't understand – you see, my wife is missing."

Looking at me like he thought I was crazy, Bob said, "Missing?"

"Yes. The police are investigating – she may've even been kidnapped."

"I really don't want to hear any more of this," he said. "I made my decision and that's final."

"You don't believe me? Call the police and ask them."

"Come on, Richard."

"Is it because of Jim Turner's account? I'll call him right now and explain everything. I'll –"

"That won't be necessary."

"This isn't fair," I said.

"Fair?" Bob said. "I think I've been incredibly fair with you. I don't think anyone else in my situation would have been nearly as fair as I've been. I've given you every opportunity to succeed at this company. We even opened the door for a possible promotion and it didn't make a difference. You tell me you're at appointments that don't exist, you clock in late and leave early, you take two-hour lunches, you fall behind on all of your projects. If that's not enough, you're a suspect in a murder case, you show up here beaten and bruised with ridiculous stories. Then, today, Steve tells me you accuse him of sending you threatening emails –"

"Is that why you're firing me?" I said, "because of

what Steve said?"

"No, this has nothing to do with Steve, this has to do with you, Richard. I still think you're a good guy, but you obviously have some problems in your life right now. If I were you, I'd take some time to solve them."

"How could you trust Steve?" I said desperately. "He's not a Jew!"

Bob was shaking his head.

"Just leave, Richard. Before I really start to get upset."

At my cubicle, I gathered some personal items and put them in a box. I included a Zip disk that had information about my clients and prospects. Technically, I was breaking the law because I had signed an agreement when I started working for Midtown Consulting that all my leads and clients were the company's permanent property, but there was no way I was going to leave empty-handed.

Word of my firing must have spread quickly, because I noticed how people were trying to steer clear of me. Carrying my box of belongings, I headed down the long corridor toward the exit, noticing the heads of several secretaries and other workers peering over their cubicles to watch my departure. They probably couldn't wait until I was gone, so they could start gossiping about me – "Richard Segal was fired."… "Did you hear the big news? Richard Segal was fired today." Then after they left work they would talk about it over dinner – "Remember that guy I told you about, Richard Segal? You know, the one who was questioned about a murder? Well, he showed up today all beaten up, then he was fired. Yep, it's true. And get this – now he says his wife is missing. Is there something really weird about that guy or what?" I even thought I heard one of the secretaries starting to giggle.

Then Steve Ferguson appeared, heading toward me. He must have left one of the offices along the corridor while I was engrossed in thought because I didn't notice him until we were about five yards apart.

As we passed each other, he said, "Good luck, Richard," in a typically backhanded way, with absolutely no sincerity. The next moment I had dropped the box on the floor and was charging him. I caught him by surprise and punched him on the back of his head. He fell to the floor on his knees. Secretaries were shrieking. I kept going, punching Steve's head.

It seemed like a few seconds later I was walking fast along Forty-eighth Street, toward Fifth Avenue. Leaving the office and the building had happened in a daze. I couldn't believe what I had just done. Not only had I beaten up an ex-coworker in plain view of an office full of witnesses, but I had left behind the box that included information about all of my prospects and clients. Now when I started looking for a new job I would have nothing to offer a prospective company. After the scene I had caused there was no way I could ever ask Bob or anyone else at Midtown for a recommendation. Knowing Steve, he was probably going to press criminal charges against me. That was all I needed in my life right now – more trouble with the police.

It was misting and the streets were wet. Crossing Fifth Avenue and Forty-eighth Street, the same intersection where I had originally spotted Michael Rudnick, I noticed a black Volkswagen bug passing by and I heard Rudnick Jr.'s voice in my head saying, "Confess... or else." I wondered if I had made a mistake by letting Rudnick Jr. leave the bar without calling the police. Maybe he was as psychotic as his father and had kidnapped Paula and was holding her hostage somewhere. The way he had beaten me up definitely showed he had a violent streak. If I hadn't been in such a rush to get back to Manhattan, maybe I could have found out where he was keeping her.

On Park Avenue, I spotted *another* black bug. This one was driven by a black guy with gray hair, but I thought that the man driving the first bug had been white. Then I spotted yet another black bug on Lexington. The driver of this bug was a young woman with straight dark hair. I ran across the street and banged on the driver-side window with my fists. The woman looked at me like I was insane. Then I heard Michael Rudnick's teenaged voice say, "You're gonna feel it! You're gonna feel it!" Pounding on the windshield, I shouted, "Shut up! Shut the hell up!" The traffic broke and the woman drove away. I started to chase after her until I realized what I was doing. I returned to the sidewalk and stood under an awning, feeling dizzy and nauseous. A man asked me if I was all right and I screamed at him to get the hell away from me. I leaned over with my hands against my knees until I caught my breath, then I continued home.

I washed my face with cold water and soothed my sore hand with a package of frozen peas. My ribs and hands were still throbbing, but I didn't think I had broken any bones.

There were no messages on my answering machine. I called the local precinct and left a message on Detective Himoto's voicemail:

"Hello, this is Richard Segal. Check out a teenager named Rudnick in Cranbury, New Jersey. It's a long story, but his father, Michael Rudnick, was murdered a couple of weeks ago, and I think he might've kidnapped Paula in revenge. Call me if you have any questions."

I hung up, suddenly certain that Paula was dead.

Otis had been barking at me since I'd come home. I didn't feel like locking him up, so I just ignored him, figuring he would shut up eventually.

I had a splitting headache and my knuckles were hurting again. I went into the kitchen to take a couple of Tylenols and to put the frozen peas back on my hand, when I noticed that Otis's dish was empty. I hadn't fed him since yesterday morning, which explained why he was acting so crazy. I took out a can of Alpo from the cabinet and opened the drawer to get the can opener. I started to close the drawer when I realized that something was wrong. I took deep breaths, trying to stay calm. But then I checked the dishwasher and the other drawers and I realized that there was no mistake – the butcher knife was definitely gone.

My mind was swirling with possibilities, but only one made sense – the police must have broken into my apartment and taken the knife as evidence.

I checked the front door, but there was no sign of a break-in. I called Raymond on the intercom and he said that as far as he knew no one had used the spare key.

Maybe Raymond was lying, covering for the police.

Frantically, I checked the drawer again, emptying everything onto the counter. I searched the entire kitchen, including the garbage, but there was no butcher knife anywhere. The police were probably testing it at a lab for Michael Rudnick's blood. Maybe they had installed secret cameras in the apartment and were watching me. I checked the kitchen, the living room, and the dining room, but I couldn't find a camera anywhere.

Suddenly, I remembered exactly where the knife was – it was in the bedroom, of course.

I went into the bedroom and started searching through the drawers in the dresser and the night table. Otis had followed me and he was barking like he was rabid, facing the door to Paula's closet.

The closet was in the corner of the room, next to the bathroom, and I almost never went in there. I took a few steps forward and then I stopped, smelling a strange odor. It reminded me of when Paula and I had first moved to New York after college. We had lived in a run-down walk-up on Amsterdam Avenue and the landlord had put down mouse poison. Afterwards, there was a nauseating odor in the walls for months.

But this odor was worse than dead mice.

Otis was growling and Michael Rudnick was laughing as I saw Paula and myself fighting in the bedroom. I was drunk, threatening her with the butcher knife, shouting, "Where's your lover boy?! Where is he?!"

Then, staring at the closet door, I heard Michael Rudnick saying, "You're gonna feel it. You're gonna feel it." His voice was so loud and clear, it sounded like it was coming from inside my head.

"Shut up!" I yelled. "Shut up!"

But he continued – "You're gonna feel it. You're gonna feel it" – and then I saw Paula, scratching my face, digging her nails into my skin as I came at her with the knife. I had another flashback – seeing droplets of blood on the floor near the closet the other day. I'd assumed the blood had come from me.

I turned the knob slowly, opening the door a crack. An odor rushed out, so nauseating I almost fainted. Then I opened the door all the way and gagged. Paula's bloated, upright body was facing me, wedged between the racks of clothing. The butcher knife was still in her chest and her wide-open eyes were staring right at me.

I stumbled backwards, falling away from the closet. Otis was barking louder than I had ever heard a dog bark. The noise was screeching, stinging my ears.

I rushed into the bathroom and threw up onto the floor. Then I returned to the bedroom, hoping that I had been hallucinating. But Paula was still there, with the knife in her chest and those cold, staring eyes.

Otis followed me down the hallway, still barking like crazy. There had to be some mistake – I couldn't have killed my wife. Rudnick Jr. must have broken into the apartment somehow and killed Paula with the knife I'd used to kill his father. Or maybe Doug did it. Tuesday night, Doug could have come back to the apartment and stabbed Paula while I was passed out drunk.

I picked up the phone in the kitchen and dialed 911. When the operator answered I realized that there was no way the police would ever believe that Doug or Rudnick Jr. had murdered Paula when I didn't believe it myself.

"Hello?" the female operator said. "Is anyone there? *Hello.*"

"Yes," I said, suddenly numb. "I'm here."

"Would you like to report an emergency?"

"No, I'd like to report a murder," I said.

"A murder?"

"Yes," I said. "My name's Richard Segal and I murdered my wife."

I explained that the police could find Paula's body where I had left it, in the bedroom closet, and then I gave the operator my address and apartment number. She wanted me to stay on the line with her until the police arrived, but I said I had to go.

I had a glass of cold water in the kitchen, then I went out to the terrace. It was still misting and there was a cool breeze against my face.

I climbed onto the railing and took a deep breath. I looked down at the spinning sidewalk and saw Paula waiting for me.

I closed my eyes. The next moment, I was falling, so fast my face felt like it was going to explode. Then I hit the ground, with a loud *crack*.

I opened my eyes. Blurry feet were gathered around me and voices were telling me to "stay still," and that everything was going to be "okay."

Now there were horrible, excruciating pains in my legs and arms and all through my back and neck.

Paula was kneeling next to me.

"Paula," I mumbled. "Paula…"

I tried to get up, dazed and bloodied, but someone held me down.

"Paula," I said. "Paula…"

But she was gone. There were just strangers around me:

"Where'd he jump from?"

"I don't know."

"I saw it – the fifth floor."

"The *fifth* floor – damn."

"Shit, look at his face."

"Man, the poor guy."

"Don't worry, pal. You're gonna be just fine."

About Us

In addition to No Exit Press, Oldcastle Books has a number of other imprints, including Kamera Books, Creative Essentials, Pulp! The Classics, Pocket Essentials and High Stakes Publishing > oldcastlebooks.co.uk

For more information about Crime Books go to > crimetime. co.uk

Check out the kamera film salon for independent, arthouse and world cinema > kamera.co.uk

For more information, media enquiries and review copies please contact Frances > frances@oldcastlebooks.com